HARD TEAMWORK

Bo Simmons had a few little faults. He liked to booze and he liked to brawl. That's why his brother Buck ran the huge Simmons ranch, and Bo did not.

On the other hand, when it came to a fight to the death, Bo was the one that Canyon O'Grady wanted to have on his side.

That was just where Bo was as Will Purdue's riders poured into town.

Both Bo and O'Grady had their guns out as they faced the private army that Purdue had sent to end the range war once and for all. The only question was which of them would make the first kill . . . and whether either of them would come out of this bloody battle against bad men and bad odds alive. . . .

JON SHARPE'S
CANYON O'GRADY
RIDES ON

CANYON O'GRADY

25

ROCKY MOUNTAIN FEUD

by
Jon Sharpe

A SIGNET BOOK

SIGNET
Published by the Penguin Group
Penguin Books USA Inc., 375 Hudson Street,
New York, New York 10014, U.S.A.
Penguin Books Ltd, 27 Wrights Lane,
London W8 5TZ, England
Penguin Books Australia Ltd, Ringwood,
Victoria, Australia
Penguin Books Canada Ltd, 10 Alcorn Avenue,
Toronto, Ontario, Canada M4V 3B2
Penguin Books (N.Z.) Ltd, 182–190 Wairau Road,
Auckland 10, New Zealand

Penguin Books Ltd, Registered Offices:
Harmondsworth, Middlesex, England

First published by Signet, an imprint of New American Library,
a division of Penguin Books USA Inc.

First Printing, May, 1993
10 9 8 7 6 5 4 3 2

 REGISTERED TRADEMARK—MARCA REGISTRADA

Printed in Canada

Canyon O'Grady

His was a heritage of blackguards and poets, fighters and lovers, men who could draw a pistol and bed a lass with the same ease.

Freedom was a cry seared into Canyon O'Grady, justice a banner of the heart.

With the great wave of those who fled to America, the new land of hope and heartbreak, solace and savagery, he came to ride the untamed wilderness of the Old West.

With a smile or a six-gun, Canyon O'Grady became a name feared by some and welcomed by others but remembered by all. . . .

Colorado Territory, 1861, where disputes usually adjudicated by the law were often settled with violence and bloodshed . . .

1

Canyon O'Grady had received some strange orders during his time as a member of the United States Secret Service, but none so strange or cryptic as the message he received by telegraph on his last day in Peyton Springs, Arkansas.

He woke that morning with Polly Monroe. Polly was a dark-haired gal in her mid-twenties, full-bodied and eager to please. She was lying on her back, and her big breasts had flattened out a bit. O'Grady studied her for a few moments. He thought that by the time she reached forty she'd probably be fat. Maybe that was unkind. Maybe she'd be a handsome, plump schoolmarm. Since she had taken over as Peyton Springs' teacher more fathers were taking their kids to school. This was her own observation. Polly *knew* that the fathers came to see her. It made her nervous, she said. It made her frightened that she might lose her job if the town *mothers* got it into their heads that their husbands were spending too much time at the schoolhouse.

O'Grady had noticed Polly Monroe as soon as he arrived in town, but it was only last night—after he'd been there a week—that she had come to his room.

He'd been pleasantly surprised when he opened the

door to his hotel room and saw her standing out in the hall. She was wringing her hands nervously, looking up and down the hall.

"I'm sorry," she said. "This is silly, but can I come in?"

"Sure," he said, stepping back.

Inside the room she seemed to grow less nervous rather than more so. He found that strange. After all, he *had* been pursuing her—after a fashion—since his arrival in town. Oh, he hadn't been . . . *obnoxious* about it, or particularly pushy, but he had certainly let her know of his interest. So he found it odd that she seemed calm while alone in his room with him.

"You're probably wondering why I came here," she said.

"I am, yes."

"Well, to tell you the truth," she said, "so am I. I mean, I *know* why I'm here. I'm just surprised that I got up the nerve to come."

"Well," he said, "since you know why you're here, maybe you'd like to tell me."

"Oh," she said, meeting his eyes with a bold gaze, "I think you know, Canyon O'Grady. You've made no secret of the fact that you . . . want me."

"And you've made no secret of the fact that you want no part of me," he said. "I guess that makes us even."

"No," she said, "no, you don't understand. It's not that I have no interest."

"You do?"

"Well . . . yes, I do. Of course I do. I find you very attractive."

"You could have fooled me," he said.

"Well, I *have* been trying to fool someone," she said, "but not you."

"Who then?"

"Well . . . me, I suppose, and the townspeople."

"The townspeople?"

"I've been worried, you see," she said. "I mean, I wouldn't want them to think that their schoolteacher was a *loose* woman. I mean, taking up with a stranger who came to town."

"I see," he said. "Well, I suspected it was something like that. Thank you for coming here to clear it up."

"Well . . . I came to clear something up, but that wasn't it."

"What is it, then?"

"Oh, Canyon," she said, shaking her head. She was using the tone she used on her younger children when she was scolding them for not knowing something she thought they should know.

"You don't mean . . ."

"Yes," she said, "I do." She giggled and said, "I came in the back way so no one would see me."

"Polly," he said, stepping closer to her, "are you sure?"

"Oh, yes," she said, "I'm *very* sure. I mean, I *think* I'm very sure. It might help me truly decide if you would . . . kiss me."

He took her by the shoulders then and leaned down and kissed her lips—gently at first, then more insistently. Her lips parted and he passed his tongue between them. She moaned and closed her hands over his biceps.

"Did that help?" he asked, moving his head back

so that she could speak, even though his lips were still touching hers.

"Oh . . . oh yes," she said, breathlessly. "That helped quite a lot."

"And you're still sure?"

"I'm *very* sure," she said, and kissed him hungrily. . . .

The first time they made love it was quickly, eagerly, both groaning and breathing heavily, both anxious to see what it would be like, exploring each other with hands and lips. He lifted her breasts to his mouth and licked and sucked her large nipples. She closed her hands over his erect penis, gasping as she did. She stroked him at first, and then pulled on him insistently, lifting her hips, until he was buried inside of her.

"Oh God, yes," she moaned, tears forming in the corners of her eyes.

He drove into her, sliding his hands beneath her to cup her big buttocks and pull her to him with each thrust. She was a big girl, and soon they were bouncing on the bed so hard that it was actually hopping up off the floor every so often. Whoever had the room beneath them must have been curious about what was going on. Hopefully, though, they wouldn't come up and complain. . . .

The second time they made love it was easier, slower, more gentle. He was on top again, but this time when he entered her it was sweet and easy. She wrapped her heavy thighs around his hips and closed her eyes as he moved in and out of her in long, easy strokes. She moaned and sighed and reached up to grasp the brass bedposts. He ducked his head to lick and suck her nipples while he was still inside of her, and then worked his way up so he could lick the salty sweat from her neck.

"Oh Canyon, yes, oh yes," she murmured, moving her hips in unison with his. "Oh God, if I had missed this . . ."

Funny. He was thinking the same thing. . . .

Now, with the morning light streaming in through the window, he leaned over and licked first one nipple, then the other. She moaned, stirred, but didn't wake. He continued to kiss her breasts and slid his hand beneath the sheet. He ran his fingers through the thick tangle of hair between her legs, found her moistness, and slid one finger inside. She came awake then, her eyes opening suddenly and widening. She bit her lips as he moved his finger around inside of her, and then she laughed, a strange, bawdy laugh he would not have thought her capable of before this night.

"Oh my, Canyon!" she exclaimed happily, lifting her hips against the pressure of his hand. "I'm so glad I came last night. I mean, if I had missed this, *deprived* myself of this . . ."

"You would never have known," he said, finishing for her.

"And that would have been even worse," she said.

Suddenly, she reached down and took hold of his wrist.

"I want to be on top this time," she said, anxiously. "Is that . . . wicked?"

"No," he said, smiling, "not at all. By all means, let's have you on top. . . ."

*　　*　　*

They were resting an hour later when there was a knock on his door.

"Who's that?" she asked, grabbing the sheet and pulling it up to her neck.

"Easy," he said to her, gently, "take it easy."

"Don't answer it," she said in a husky whisper.

The knock came again.

"Who is it?" he called out this time.

"Mr. O'Grady?"

"That's right."

"I got an important telegraph message for you, sir," the voice said.

"Slip it under the door."

There was a moment of silence, and then the voice said, "It's supposed to be important, sir. Urgent, even."

"Don't open the door!" she whispered, grabbing his arm as he put his feet on the floor.

"He's waiting for a tip," he said.

He walked to the door and said, "I'm not dressed." He slid a dollar bill beneath the door and said, "Pass the telegraph message underneath."

"Yes, sir," the voice said. The bill disappeared and a yellow piece of paper appeared. "Thank you, sir."

O'Grady picked up the piece of paper and carried it back to the bed.

"I know I'm being silly," Polly said, "but my job . . ."

"I know, honey," he said. "It's all right."

"What is that?" she asked. "*Is* it important?"

He unfolded it and read it.

"Yes," he said, "it could be important." He turned to look at her and said, "I have to leave, Polly."

"Now?" she asked. "Today?"

"Yes," he said, "today."

"Ohhh . . ." she moaned, pushing her bottom lip out prettily. "I wasted so much time, didn't I?"

"Well . . . I think we made up for it tonight, don't you?"

She slid her hand around his hip and into his lap and said, "Not *yet* we haven't. Do you have to leave *right* now?"

"Well," he said, looking down at her hand, "not *right* now. . . ."

Later, he walked Cormac out of the livery stable and mounted up. Before starting off he took the telegraph message out of his pocket and read it again. It read:

YOU HAVE TWO WEEKS TO GET TO HASTINGS, COLORADO. FURTHER INSTRUCTIONS WHEN YOU GET THERE.
WHEELER.

Major General Rufus Wheeler was his immediate superior, and he had received a lot of messages from the man over the years. This was the first time, however, that the instructions had left him so much in the dark. Two weeks to get to a town he had never heard of, to do . . . what?

Obviously, he'd find out when he got there.

2

When Canyon O'Grady rode into the town of Eli's Crossing, he knew he still had two days of riding ahead of him to get to Hastings. However, he had four days in which to do it, so he decided to stop in Eli's Crossing for a hot meal and a soft bed—and maybe a warm woman—before continuing on. He'd also been pushing Cormac hard to make his two-week deadline. The horse could use some rest.

During his ride through town to the livery he found Eli's Crossing to be a classic example of a small town with visions of growing larger. For now it had one hotel, one saloon, and a bank, but construction had been started on two of three new buildings, and it made sense that another hotel or saloon was in the works.

When he'd found the livery he dismounted and walked Cormac inside. A young man with bony shoulders and long legs, wiping his hands on a dirty cloth, almost ran into him. He stopped short to avoid the collision.

"Oh, sorry!" the young man exclaimed. "I meant to come out when I heard you ride up."

"No problem," O'Grady said. He handed over Cormac's reins and said, "I've been pushing him pretty hard the past week or so. Take good care of him. We'll be riding again in the morning."

"I'll treat him good, mister," the man said. His jaw was so smooth O'Grady doubted that he had started shaving yet. He looked about twenty, still more boy than man.

O'Grady collected his rifle and saddlebags and said, "Looks like a quiet little town."

"Won't be little for long," the young man said. "Buildin' us another hotel and another saloon. We're growin'."

"That's good," O'Grady said. "Thanks for taking care of him."

"Sure, mister."

O'Grady tossed his saddlebags over his shoulder and headed for the hotel.

The Simmons ranch was an hour's ride outside of Eli's Crossing. The ranch was owned by Buck Simmons, and the foreman was his younger brother, Bo. Everyone on the ranch knew, however, that Bo worked *for* Buck, even though the two men were brothers. What they all found odd was that Bo didn't seem to mind the arrangement.

There were men on the ranch who thought that if it was *their* brother who owned a ranch that he would *give* them a piece of it. When Bo heard that talk he called the men together in the bunkhouse and laid it out for them.

"I ain't never been gave nothin' I didn't work for," he told them, "and I ain't about to start now. My brother Buck built this place with his own two hands while I was out sowing my wild oats." Bo didn't really know what that meant, but it's what Buck used to say to him years ago, that he was out "sowing his wild oats." "I came here and my brother gave me a job. Now I work for what I get, and I don't want any of you yahoos thinkin' different, okay?"

The men nodded and said they understood, and now the talk behind Buck and Bo's back was still there, but there was less of it.

Buck Simmons was forty-five years old, a big man with a barrel chest and a head of steel-gray hair. His wife, however, was considerably younger, a beautiful, dark-haired Mexican woman of twenty-four whose father was very happy with the union between Buck Simmons and his daughter, Valeria.

Bo Simmons was thirty-eight, but he had led a hard life and looked at least as old as his brother. He was smaller in stature, but built along the same general lines. His hair was black and gray in equal parts. He was known to be a fast man with a gun or his fists, and more than once he'd had to back up his word with either/or. When he did so he did it without hesitation. He did not have the flash temper of his youth, but neither did he have his brother's much longer fuse.

Valeria Manolito Simmons was Buck's second wife. His first had died several years earlier, killed more by hard work than anything else—at least, that was what Buck always thought. She had not been a physically strong woman, and the demands of being his wife had finally done her in. Bo told Buck he was crazy to think that, but he had never been able to change his brother's mind.

From that first marriage, Buck Simmons had a son and a daughter. His son, Mark, was twenty-two, and someday Buck hoped to turn the ranch over to him. To date, however, Mark did not display the same strength of character that his father did—or, for that matter, that his older sister did. If Julia Simmons, twenty-six, had been a man, Buck would have had no qualms about turning the ranch over to her. She was a strong woman, and would have run the ranch with an iron hand.

The other problem was that Mark, who had first resented Valeria for taking his mother's place, now became moon-eyed and nervous whenever he was around her. He stammered and stuttered when he tried to talk to her. She thought it was sweet, Buck thought it was damned odd, Bo thought it was silly, and Julia thought it meant that her brother was in love with their stepmother.

Julia, while she resembled her late mother strongly, had more physical strength and stamina than her mother had ever had. She loved her father and her uncle and her brother but was rather indifferent toward Valeria, even after two years of marriage to her father.

Buck said that Julia was the smartest member of the family, and that it wasn't only because he had sent her to school back east. He said she was just naturally smart, and had the "common sense God gave a man." Julia was secretly pleased that God had given her the "common sense of a woman."

Buck Simmons was sitting at his desk, frowning over the accounts, when his daughter entered his study. She walked to him and kissed the top of his head, then looked down at the mass of paper on his desk.

"Problems?" she asked.

He looked up at her and tried—unsuccessfully—to smile. Instead, he patted her hand and frowned.

"I won't lie to you, girl," he said. "Things are not

going as well as I would like, and the bank isn't being very understanding."

"Well, we know why that is, Pa," she said, putting her hand on his shoulder. "That snake Will Purdue is after everything we have."

"I know, Julia," Buck said, "and that includes you, don't it?"

"Will doesn't want me, Pa," she said. "He just wants what you have, and I'm one of those things."

"I think he's in love with you."

"Well I'm not in love with *him*, Pa, and I never will be," she said.

"You could do worse, gal," he said. "Lord knows, *he* couldn't do better."

"Forget it, Pa."

"He's handsome, rich, and—"

"I got work to do," she said, storming away from his desk. "I'll see you for dinner, Pa."

On the way out, she passed Valeria and acknowledged her with a nod.

Buck, seeing his wife enter the room, got up and hurried around his desk. He embraced her and kissed her forehead. She was so beautiful that his heart ached every time he looked at her. Her long black hair was swept back from her smooth forehead today, and her black eyes held a worried look.

"I brought you some coffee, husband," she said, handing him the cup.

"Thank you, Val," he said. He was the only person in the world who called her Val.

"Are things not going well?" she asked, giving him a worried look.

"Things are going just fine, dear," he said. "You

go on back to your work, now, and I'll go to mine, hmm?"

"Yes, my husband."

Still looking worried, she turned and left.

Buck returned to his desk. He had no qualms about telling the truth to Julia, but he tried to keep his business affairs away from Valeria. She wouldn't understand, and she'd worry much too much. Worrying was *his* job.

Julia was right. Will Purdue *was* pushing, and he was using the bank to do it. Buck was a little behind on payments, and the bank was being insistent about wanting them. Also, he had some creditors who were pushing him, and he felt that that too was Will Purdue's doing.

In reality, Buck's ranch was larger than Purdue's—physically larger. He had more land and more grazing ground, and more water, which was why Purdue wanted it. Purdue, however, was more successful, richer. Being a rich man, he had much more ammunition to throw against Buck than Buck had any right to think he could withstand. Both of the Simmons brothers, however, were stubborn, and were not about to give in to Will Purdue's pressure tactics.

"And if he wants us to start pushing back," Bo Simmons had told his brother more than once, "we can do that, too."

Buck knew he could do that, but he also knew that doing that could escalate into a full-fledged range war. He had seen range wars before, and it was rare that *anyone* came out a winner.

Still, he wasn't about to let Will Purdue sweep down on him and take away everything he had built.

Not a chance.

3

O'Grady registered at the hotel and made arrangements for a bath. He soaked in the hot water until it got tepid, then stepped out of the tub and dressed in fresh clothing. Feeling like a new man, he left the hotel and walked over to the saloon.

It was late afternoon by then, and the saloon was almost three-quarters full. There were still some tables with empty chairs, and a few spots at the bar. O'Grady claimed one of the spaces at the bar and ordered a beer.

"Just get into town?" the bartender asked, setting the beer down in front of him.

"A little while ago," O'Grady said.

"Passin' through?"

"That's right."

"Be a nice place to settle down," the bartender said. "Town's startin' to grow."

"Yeah," a man at the bar said, "thanks to Will Purdue."

"Is that right?" O'Grady commented.

The man who had spoken turned and looked at him.

"You don't think so, mister?"

O'Grady looked at the man in surprise, still holding his beer in his left hand.

"Are you talking to me?" he asked.

"That's right," the man said. He was a burly man with a heavy beard that looked like it hadn't been cleaned in a few days. "You don't think that Mr. Purdue is helping this town grow?"

"You work for Mr. Purdue?" O'Grady asked.

"That's right."

"Well, I'll tell you the truth, mister," O'Grady said, "I never heard of Will Purdue, so I don't guess I can comment on whether he's helping the town grow or not."

"Hey, Pete," one of the other men at the bar said. "Forget it."

"No," Pete said to his friend, "I don't want to forget it." He faced O'Grady again and said, "You sayin' you can't take my word for it?"

O'Grady gave the man an exasperated look.

"Look, friend," he said, "all I want to do is drink my beer, all right? I didn't come in here looking for an argument, certainly not about some man I never even heard of."

"You sayin' Mr. Purdue is nobody, just because you ain't heard of him?" the man called Pete asked.

"Hey!" O'Grady said, growing annoyed. "If you're looking for an argument, go look somewhere else, okay? I've got nothing to say on the subject."

He turned to the bar with his beer, looking away from the man at the bartender. At the same time he saw the bartender's eyes widen as he watched the man named Pete.

O'Grady moved quickly, sidestepping and avoiding the blow Pete had aimed at his head with his fist. As the fist moved by him, O'Grady threw the beer into Pete's face, and followed with his own punch. He caught Pete flush on the jaw, driving the man back along the bar. Others moved out of his way as the man fought for his balance and lost, finally stumbling to the floor.

"Give me another beer, bartender," O'Grady said. "I seem to have spilled that one."

"Sure, friend," the bartender said.

O'Grady looked at some of the other men who were standing at the bar.

"Any of you friends of this fella's?"

"Yeah," one of them said, "we work with him."

"Well, you better get him out of here," O'Grady said. "He seems to be looking for a fight, and I'm not in the mood."

"Sure, pal," another man said.

Two men bent down and put their hands under Pete's arms, lifting him to his feet. Pete was sputtering from the beer, and his head was still reeling from the punch.

"You throw a pretty nice punch, mister," the bartender said.

"Thanks," O'Grady said, "and thanks for your help."

"My help?" the bartender asked, looking confused.

"Sure," O'Grady said, "you were watching him and I was watching you. When he made his move, I knew it by the look on your face."

"Is that right?" the bartender said. "Huh! I was wondering how you knew his punch was comin', when you wasn't even lookin' at him. It was that easy, huh?"

"It was that easy."

O'Grady lifted his beer to drink from it and sensed a presence next to him. He turned and saw a woman standing there. She was young, in her twenties, and he hadn't seen her when he came in. From the dress she was wearing, vivid red and low-cut, he knew she worked there.

"Hello," she said.

"Hi," he said. "I didn't see you when I first came in. Must be something wrong with my eyes."

"I wasn't here when you first came in," she said. "I came in just as you were, uh, taking care of Pete. Thanks for the compliment, though."

He was sure she received plenty of compliments. She had black hair that hung down to pale shoulders, and a creamy, firm cleavage.

"Len," she said to the bartender, "give the man another beer, on the house."

O'Grady drained the one he had and set the empty mug down on the bar.

"I appreciate that," he said, "but isn't your boss going to mind you giving away his beer?"

"I don't think the boss will mind," she said.

The bartender brought over a fresh beer, looked at the woman, and said, "Somethin' for you, boss?"

"Whiskey, Len," she said.

Len nodded and poured her shot.

O'Grady turned, to face her full-on and study her. "*You're* the boss?"

"That's right," she said, lifting her drink. "Here's to your health."

They clinked glasses and drank, he draining half the beer, she finishing off the whiskey with a quick move.

"I was impressed with the way you handled Pete," she said.

"I assume he's a regular in here?"

"Oh sure," she said. "He's in here every night, usually tries to pick a fight."

"Does he usually get any takers?"

"Sometimes," she said, "if it's somebody who doesn't know any better."

"I guess he usually wins."

"Oh yeah," she said. "I've never seen him lose, especially not to one punch."

"I guess I got lucky," he said.

"Oh," she said, "I doubt that. You plan on being in town long?"

"I hadn't, no," O'Grady said, looking at her regretfully. "I have a pressing appointment elsewhere."

"Oh, that's too bad," she said. "Well, maybe you can stop in on your way *back* from your pressing appointment?"

"Might be I could, yes," he said.

"My name is Cora."

She put her hand out like a man's, to shake, and he did, finding her grip firm.

"Canyon O'Grady."

"Canyon, huh?" she said. "Nice name."

"Thanks."

She looked him up and down in a frank appraisal and then said, "Well, enjoy yourself in my place tonight. If you stay long enough, the house will buy you another." She looked at Len, to make sure he was listening.

"Sure," Len said, nodding.

"Thank you, Cora."

She nodded, smiled, and then turned and began to circulate, checking on her customers.

"Cora likes you," Len said.

26

"Think so?" O'Grady asked, leaning on the bar. He could follow her progress in the mirror behind the bar.

"Oh, I *know* so," Len said. "She don't usually talk to strangers much."

"Maybe she's just grateful that I managed to get Pete out of here before he did some damage."

Len frowned.

"How did you know that he causes damage when he fights?"

"Big man like that," O'Grady said, "he's got to break something when he gets into a fight."

"Yeah," another man at the bar said. "I seen Peter break arms, legs, jaws even. I was you, mister, I'd be careful walkin' back to my hotel tonight."

O'Grady looked over at the man, who spoke with a good-natured expression on his face.

"Thanks for the warning."

"My pleasure," the man said. He turned to face O'Grady and stuck out his hand. "Name's Vince Gill."

"Mr. Gill," O'Grady said, shaking hands.

"Heard you say your name," Gill said. "O'Grady, that's Irish, right?"

"That's right."

"Knew an Irishman once," Gill said. "He was a good fighter—kind of like you."

"I don't like to fight," O'Grady said. "I only do it when I have no choice."

"I could see that," Gill said, as both men turned to lean on the bar again. "You did what you could to avoid a fight, but Pete—that's Pete Webber—just wasn't lettin' you off."

"Too bad," O'Grady said. "All I wanted was a couple of quiet beers, and then a good night's sleep before I move on."

"So you're, uh, not lookin' for work around here?" Gill asked.

"No," O'Grady said. "I have to be moving on in the morning."

"Cause if you were," Gill said, "I know a ranch that's always lookin' for good men."

"Is that right?"

"The Simmons ranch," Gill said. "That's where I work, for Big Buck Simmons."

Gill said it as if he were very proud of the fact that he worked for this man Simmons.

"I'm not going to have to fight *you* if I say I never heard of Buck Simmons, am I?"

Gill laughed and said, "No, you won't. In fact, you got another free beer comin', compliments of Big Buck Simmons. How's that?"

O'Grady smiled and said, "I'll take it."

4

Will Purdue looked across his desk at the manager of the Bank of Eli's Crossing. The banker, David Beekman, was looking all around the room, focusing his eyes on anything that would keep him from having to look back at Purdue.

"It's taking too long, David," Purdue said. "I want that land."

"Mr. Purdue," Beekman said, "Buck Simmons has been a depositor in the bank a long time. I can't just . . . *take* his land without giving him an opportunity to pay what he owes."

"You don't have to give him so goddamned *many* extensions, David," Purdue said, impatiently.

"Mr. Purdue," Beekman said, "I . . . I'm just giving him what I would give any other depositor. A fair chance to settle his—"

Purdue leaned forward in his chair, and the movement alone cut off what the banker was saying.

"Don't forget that *I* am a depositor in the bank, too, Beekman," Purdue said.

"I know that, sir."

"Do you know what would happen to your bank if I pulled all of my money out?"

Beekman started to sweat. He was a fat man, and

when he sweated he smelled. Purdue wrinkled his nose and sat back in his chair to get away from the stink.

"It isn't a very pleasant thought, Mr. Purdue," Beekman said. To himself he thought that if Purdue did take his money out of the Eli's Crossing bank, he would have to go a long way to deposit it into another bank. That would be inconvenient for Purdue, and Beekman knew that the other man didn't like being inconvenienced.

He held on to that thought.

Purdue wrinkled his nose again. Leaning back had not gotten him far enough away from Beekman.

"All right, Beekman," Purdue said, "get out. Go back to your bank."

"Yes, Mr. Purdue."

"But be warned," Purdue said as the fat man waddled toward the door, "at the first opportunity I want you to foreclose on those loans. Do you understand?"

Beekman turned and said, "Yessir, I understand, Mr. Purdue."

As Beekman left Purdue's study the rancher stood up, turned, and opened the window behind his desk. Immediately fresh air flowed into the room, dispelling the smell of the fat man.

Purdue was tall and lean, in his late thirties, and he could never understand why a man—like Beekman— would let himself get so fat. Purdue liked women, and he knew that if he was fat he would still be able to get all the women he wanted because of his money, but he enjoyed women too much to want to pay them—or force them—to accept his company. When he was with a woman he liked knowing that she was enjoying him as much as he was enjoying her, and that it had nothing to do with his money—well, almost nothing.

He turned, hearing someone enter the room.

"Mr. Purdue."

It was his foreman, Larry Rhodes. Rhodes was Purdue's age, and had been with Purdue a long time. If not for the fact that Purdue was the employer and Rhodes the employee, Purdue almost thought they could be friends.

"Yes, Rhodes?"

"I, uh, saw Beekman leave," Rhodes said. "I was just curious. . . ."

"No action yet, Larry," Purdue said. He picked a pen up from his desk, and as he spoke seemed to study it. "Soon, though. The banker knows that it has to be soon."

"He was nervous," Rhodes said. "I, uh, smelled him as he was going out."

Purdue put the pen down and looked at his foreman.

"Can you still smell him in here?"

"No," Rhodes said, "no, the smell is gone now."

"Good," Purdue said. "I'd hate to think I could ever get *used* to that smell and not know that it was still in the room."

"No," Rhodes said again, "it's gone."

"Good," Purdue said. He looked at Rhodes and asked, "Is there anything else?"

"Uh, yeah. Some of the men were wondering about that, uh, party tomorrow night at the Watson place?"

"Party?" Purdue asked. "What party?"

"You know," Rhodes said, "old man Watson's daughter is gettin' engaged."

"Oh, yes, that party," Purdue said. "What about it?"

"The men were wondering if they'd be able to go to it," Rhodes said. "I mean, you know, if you'd be needing them and all. . . ."

"Oh," Purdue said, "I don't think I'll be needing them tomorrow night, Larry. Just keep a few on the grounds for security, and the rest can go."

They both knew that they weren't talking about the ranch hands, but the gunmen that Purdue employed.

"And the other men?" Rhodes asked, and this time he did mean the ranch hands.

"Sure," Purdue said, "they can go, too."

"Will, uh, you be goin'?"

"I don't know," Purdue said. "Do you suppose the Simmonses will be there?"

"I'm sure they will," Rhodes said. "In fact, I think Julia Simmons is Theresa Watson's maid of honor, or something. I'm sure *she'll* be there."

"Hmm," Purdue said, attempting to appear bored, "maybe I will stop in, just for a few minutes. You know, to pay my respects and bring a gift."

"Sure," Rhodes said, nodding.

"I guess that means I'll have to go into town tomorrow and *buy* a gift," Purdue said. "What do you buy for a woman who's getting engaged?"

"I don't know," Rhodes said. "You don't think *I'll* have to buy a gift just to, uh, go to the party, do you?"

"No, no," Purdue said. "I wouldn't worry about that if I was you. I'm only thinking of it because I'm a neighbor. You and the men won't have to worry about that. You can just go and eat, drink, and dance."

Rhodes looked relieved and said, "Yeah, that's what I thought."

"Anything else, Larry?" Purdue asked.

"Uh, no, boss, that's it," Rhodes said. "Good night."

"Good night, Larry."

As Rhodes left, Purdue turned his chair around so he could face the open window and catch the breeze full on his face.

He started to think about Julia Simmons.

It was odd that he would fall in love with a woman whose father he was trying to destroy. He *was* trying to destroy Buck Simmons, but that wasn't the reason he was trying to get his loans called in. He simply wanted the Simmons land. He had offered Buck a fair price for it time and time again, but the man was more stubborn than any mule. Buck Simmons left him no choice but to *take* the land away from him. Of course, first he would try to do so by legal—albeit underhanded—means. After that . . . Well, after that *failed* he would decide what to do next.

The other problem, of course, was getting Julia to fall in love with him even while he was plotting against her father.

If only Julia weren't so . . . so desirable as a wife. It wasn't even that she was particularly beautiful. There were other women in and around Eli's Crossing who were more beautiful than she was. Available women who would be only too happy to receive attention from him. However, they weren't Julia. They weren't as smart as she was, or as tough.

God, she wouldn't only make him a good wife, she'd make a damned good *partner*—and that was what he needed. Someone to share all of this with, someone who would understand what it had taken to

33

put it together, and someone who could take an active part in helping him keep it together, and build on it.

He needed Julia Simmons—*almost* as much as he needed her father's land.

5

Julia Simmons came downstairs from her room and saw her Uncle Bo entering the house. As always at the end of the day, Bo looked years older than he actually was. She shook her head. Her uncle couldn't have worked any harder if he *had* owned a part of the ranch. She wondered why he continued to refuse whenever her father offered him a piece of it.

"Uncle Bo," she said, reaching the bottom of the stairs.

Bo turned to look at her, and smiled.

"Hello, Julia," he said. "You look as pretty as a picture, like always."

"It's the end of the day, Uncle Bo," she said. "You look like hell, and so do I."

She went to her uncle, whom she dearly loved, and kissed him on the cheek. As always, he looked embarrassed. She remembered kissing him a lot as a child, and it had never embarrassed him then. It was only after she had grown up, probably from about fourteen on, that any show of affection from her had made him blush. She wondered why her uncle had never married. Sure, he was rough around the edges, but a sweeter man she had never known. She couldn't believe that she was the only woman in the world who saw that in him.

"Well," he said, blushing, "you got the first part of that right, anyway. Where's your pa?"

"He's in his study," she said. "Do you want the cook to make you something to eat?"

"I *could* use somethin', darlin'," he said. "Thanks. I'll be in after I talk to your pa."

"Okay, Uncle Bo."

He watched her walk away, marveling at how much she reminded him of her mother. Bo Simmons had always been a little bit in love with his brother's wife— his brother's *first* wife—but he had never let anyone know that. Of course, he'd never realized that *everyone* did know it.

He walked down the hall to his brother's study and knocked on the open door to announce his presence.

"Buck?"

His older brother looked up from his desk and beckoned him to enter. He finished writing whatever it was he was writing, then looked up again.

"You want a drink?" Buck asked.

"I sure do," Bo said.

As Buck stood up and walked to the sideboard against the wall, Bo rubbed his hand over his mouth and asked, "You ain't gonna try to give me some of that sherry stuff, are you?"

"No," Buck said, "I learned my lesson the last time you spit it out all over the place. It's too expensive to waste on you. For you it's whiskey."

Buck turned and handed his brother a shot of whiskey.

"Bless you, brother," Bo said, and tossed it off.

Buck walked back to his desk with a glass of sherry.

"Where's Julia?" he asked.

"In the kitchen," Bo said. "She's havin' Cook fix me something."

"And Mark?"

"Mark went into town with a couple of the boys, Buck," Bo said.

Buck looked up and asked, "Who did he go with?"

"Uh, Fenner and Colter."

Buck made a face.

"Troublemakers."

"They're good workers, Buck," Bo said. "A little high-spirited, maybe . . ."

"They're no good for Mark to be hanging around with, Bo."

"Mark's all growed up, Buck."

"I know, I know," Buck said, frowning. "In some ways he is, and in some he isn't. I just wish he was more like . . . like . . ."

"Like Julia?"

Buck looked at his brother and said, "All right, yes, like Julia."

"Give the boy a chance, Buck," Bo said. "He'll make it, all right."

"I hope so, Bo," Buck said. "I hope so."

"Well," Bo said, backing toward the door, "thanks for the drink. I'm gonna get somethin' to eat and then turn in."

"You're not going to town?" Buck asked, with raised eyebrows.

"Not tonight, brother," Bo said.

"Gettin' old, huh, Bo?"

"I can still outdrink you, Buck," Bo said, teasingly. "You been drinkin' too much of that sherry."

"Ha! The day you can outdrink me is the day I'll give this all up."

Bo Simmons knew better. His brother would *never* give all of this up. He meant to leave it to his children, and have them leave it to theirs.

"With that on the line, Buck," Bo said, "I wouldn't take you on."

As Bo started for the door Buck said, "See if Cook can't rustle something up for me, too, will you? I'll be in in a few minutes."

"All right, Buck," Bo said. "I'll do 'er."

As his brother left the room, Buck Simmons sat back and thought briefly about his son. It wasn't fair to the boy to keep comparing him to his sister, but he just didn't have her common sense.

Bo was right. He had to give the boy more time to prove himself.

But how *much* more? That was the question.

O'Grady was finishing his third beer and preparing to buy one for Vince Gill when the batwing doors swung open and three men walked in.

"Mark!" Gill called. "Come over here, boy! I want you to meet somebody!"

The man in the middle of the three reacted to the name and came over. He looked to be all of twenty-two or so. The other two were in their thirties, and they bellied up to the bar away from O'Grady, Gill, and the one called Mark.

"This here's Canyon O'Grady," Gill said. "Canyon, this is Mark Simmons."

"Any relation to Buck Simmons?" Canyon asked, shaking the boy's hand.

"Sure am. He's my pa," Mark said, proudly. "You heard of my pa?"

O'Grady gave Gill a sidelong glance and then said, "Who hasn't?"

At the other end of the bar, the two men Mark had walked in with ordered a bottle of whiskey and three glasses.

"Buy you a beer?" O'Grady asked.

"Come on, Mark!" one of the other men called. "We got a bottle."

"I got a drink waitin' for me," Mark said to O'Grady. "Thanks, anyway. See ya later, Vince."

"Sure thing, Mark."

Mark Simmons went over to join his two friends and the bartender brought O'Grady and Gill another beer each, for which O'Grady paid.

"Those two . . ." Gill said.

O'Grady looked down the bar at the two men, who were pouring Mark Simmons a second drink, already.

"What about them?"

"They're good workers, I guess," Gill said, "but they ain't the type young Mark should be hanging around with."

"He looks old enough to know who to be friends with," O'Grady said.

"Yeah, I know," Gill said, "he *looks* old enough, but he just hasn't got the sense God gave a jackass. Now his sister, there's a different story."

"Older? Younger?"

"Older," Gill said, "and she can ride and shoot with any man in the outfit. Hell, I think she could outfight half of them if she had to."

"But not Mark?"

Gill shook his head and said, "The boy's got a long way to go to catch up to his sister."

"She sounds like quite a woman."

"She is," Gill said, and O'Grady thought in that moment that Gill must be in love with Mark Simmons' sister.

"What's her name?"

"Julia."

"Pretty?"

"A handsome woman," Gill said. "There's prettier, Canyon, but there ain't any better. Do you know what I mean?"

"I think I do, Vince," O'Grady said, "I think I do."

Outside, across the street, Pete Webber stood in the dark watching the front doors of the saloon.

"How much longer we got to wait, Pete?" one of the three men with him asked.

"As long as I say," Webber replied, gruffly. "Nobody does that to me and gets away with it."

They had been waiting for Canyon O'Grady to come out ever since the other men had helped Webber leave the saloon. Outside in the cool air the man had revived, and refused to ride back to the ranch—not without getting even, he said.

"And now it's gonna get even more interestin'," Webber said to the others. "Did you see who just went in?"

"Weren't that Mark Simmons?" one of the men said.

"That's right," Webber said. "That's who it was. Mark Simmons."

"We don't want to mess with Mark Simmons, Pete," the third man with him said. "Uh . . . do we?"

"If we want to mess with a Simmons at all, Lester," Pete Webber said, "it's little Mark. Let's just wait here and see what happens, okay?"

The other three men looked at one another and shrugged. Since Pete Webber could have probably whipped all three of them at one time, they had no choice but to agree.

6

In the time it took O'Grady and Gill to finish their beer, Mark Simmons had gotten roaring drunk. The other two men, Gill told O'Grady, were named Harlan Fenner and Lou Colter.

"Hey, bartender!" Lou Colter called out. "Another bottle!"

It was late now, and besides O'Grady, Gill, Mark Simmons, Fenner, and Colter, there were only a few others in the place. The bartender, Len, was cleaning a glass. He looked over at Vince Gill, as if for permission.

Gill shook his head at the man and then walked down the bar to the other three men.

"I think Mark's had enough, boys, don't you?" Gill asked.

"How about Mark?" Fenner asked. He looked at Gill, and then at Mark, who was grinning stupidly. "Does Mark think Mark's had enough?"

"Hell, no!" Mark cried, waving at the air as if trying to swat something. "Bartender, bring another bottle!"

"See?" Colter said to Gill.

"What I see is that Mark's drunk," Gill said, "and he's had enough. No more for him."

"Says who?" Fenner asked.

"Says me," Gill said.

Even from where he sat, O'Grady could feel the tension in the air. He could see Gill's back, but he imagined that the man was trying to stare down Fenner and Colter.

"Well," Colter finally said, "if you think he's had enough, maybe you want to make sure he gets home safe, huh, Gill?"

"Sure, boys," Gill said, "I'll see that he gets home safely."

"Well then," Fenner said, "the boy's all yours."

He gave Mark a shove that sent him off-balance into Gill, who caught him.

"Come on," Fenner said to Colter, and the two men left the saloon.

Gill turned and looked at O'Grady.

"If you help me get him on his horse, I can take him home."

"Sure," O'Grady said. He set his empty beer mug down on the bar and said, "I'd be glad to help."

Together they walked the boy through the batwing doors outside. Cormac stood off to the right.

"That's my horse over there," Gill said, jerking his head to the left. "This one here is Mark's." Mark Simmons' horse was right in front of the doors.

"Let's get him aboard, then," O'Grady said.

"I don't *wanna* go home!" Mark protested loudly. "I wanna have some more fun!"

"Fun's over, Mark," Gill said. "Time to go home and sleep it off."

It's very difficult to put a man on a horse when he doesn't want to get on, even if he's smaller than O'Grady and Gill. They finally did get him into the

43

saddle, though, and that was when four men stepped out from the shadows across the street.

O'Grady recognized Peter Webber immediately.

"What is it?" Gill asked, seeing trouble reflected in Canyon's features. His back was to the four men, and he looked over his shoulder. He said, "Shit," under his breath.

"I ain't here for you, Gill!" Webber called out. "Just step aside! I want the big fella, there!"

"There's no need for this, Peter!" Gill insisted.

"If you don't move, Gill, you're gonna get hurt," Webber said, cutting him off.

"Go ahead," O'Grady said calmly, "move. Take the boy with you."

"No," Gill said. "I ain't leaving you to face four men alone."

"My fight," O'Grady said.

"I'm making it mine," Gill said, and he turned to face the four men. "You go ahead when you're ready, Pete, but it ain't going to be as easy as you thought. Four against two, instead of four against one."

"Four against three," Mark Simmons said, and went for his gun. He was so clumsy it spun out of his hand.

"Damn," O'Grady said, and as the men across the street drew their guns he drew his *and* reached up to push Mark Simmons out of the saddle. The shooting started as Mark hit the ground on the other side of his horse with a thud.

Gill fired before O'Grady, who lost a second or two in getting Mark out of the way. He felt a bullet tug at his sleeve and then he fired, striking Pete Webber with his first shot.

He heard Gill grunt, and the man went to one knee. O'Grady fired again, bringing another man down—

no, Webber wasn't down. He was staggering, and O'Grady fired at him again, this time putting him down on his back.

There were two men on the ground, and the other two ran off into the dark.

O'Grady holstered his gun and took hold of Vince Gill's shoulders.

"You all right?"

"Caught one. . . ." Gill said, and the pain was plain in his voice.

On the other side of Mark Simmons' horse the boy was still on the ground, and he was moaning. O'Grady didn't think he had gotten hit, but he couldn't be sure.

He turned and saw the bartender standing in the doorway of the saloon.

"Better get a doctor," he told the man. "Fast."

Even before the doctor got there, the sheriff arrived. His hair was flying wildly about his head, his shirt was open, and he had his gun in his hand. Obviously, he had been awakened from a sound sleep.

"Stop right there!" he shouted, pointing his gun at O'Grady.

The red-haired agent looked at the man calmly. He couldn't "stop right there" because he wasn't doing anything but supporting Vince Gill until the doctor could arrive.

"Just take it easy, Sheriff," O'Grady said. "It's all over."

"I want your gun, mister!" the sheriff said. "And I want it now!"

There was a groan from the general direction of Mark Simmons, which attracted the sheriff's notice.

"Who's that?"

"Mark Simmons."

"Simmons?" the lawman said. "Is he shot?"

"I don't think so," O'Grady said.

The sheriff looked into the street at the two dead men and asked, "And who's that?"

"Somebody named Pete Webber, and another man," O'Grady said.

"Webber!" the sheriff said. "He works for Will Purdue."

"That's what I understand."

"You killed him?"

"That's right," O'Grady said, "he was trying to kill—"

"That's enough, mister!" the sheriff said. "I want your gun—now!"

He was back to that.

"Jesus," O'Grady said. "Here."

He took his gun from his holster and extended it to the man, butt-first. The sheriff jumped nervously at first, then moved closer and snatched the gun from O'Grady's hand, tucking it into his belt.

"What's going on here?" another voice called out.

A tall, white-haired man in shirtsleeves appeared, carrying a black bag.

"Are you the doctor?" O'Grady asked.

"That's right," the man said. "Fletcher."

"This man's been shot," O'Grady said.

"Is that Vince Gill?" the doctor asked, frowning.

"That's him."

"Come on, mister," the sheriff said, "you're going to jail."

O'Grady figured this is what he got for being the only man who could walk away from the altercation on his own.

"Oh, stand back and relax, Zeke!" the doctor demanded, crouching by Gill. "I need this man to hold my patient steady."

"But Doc . . ."

"Why don't you check on the others, Zeke?" the doctor suggested. "Let me know if they need me, or the undertaker."

"Uh, well, sure, Doc, but when you're finished, that jasper's goin' to jail."

"You ain't about to run off, are you, son?" the doctor asked O'Grady.

"No, sir."

"He'll be here, Zeke."

O'Grady held on to Vince Gill while the doctor examined him, and at the same time he watched the sheriff check the two men in the street.

"They don't need you," the sheriff announced. "They're both dead."

"Easy, Vince," the doctor said. "Looks like you took one in the hip. Bullet's still in there." While he was working he called out to the sheriff, "There seems to be another man lying over here, on the other side of this horse, Zeke!"

"Yeah," Zeke said, and ran over. "Oh, this is young Mark Simmons."

"Is he alive?"

"Oh yeah, he's alive."

"Is he shot?" the doctor asked.

"Uh . . . no, but he sure is drunk," Zeke said, "and he might have a broken arm."

The doctor looked at O'Grady and asked, "Stranger in town?"

"That's right."

"Got yourself involved in something between the Purdue ranch and Simmons ranch, already?"

"I don't think so," O'Grady said. "It was between me and that Webber fellow."

"Ah-ha . . ." the doctor said. Louder he called out, "I need two men to take this man to my office! Come on, come on!"

Two men hurried forward and took Gill from O'Grady and the doctor. O'Grady and the doctor both stood up and faced each other.

"I'd better check on young Simmons," the doctor said. "I don't know what you thought you were getting involved in, young man, but you killed two of Will Purdue's men, and Mark Simmons ended up getting hurt."

"I *kept* him from getting killed."

At this point he was wanting at least a little bit of credit. Even the crowd that was beginning to form, seeing him as the only man unharmed, was eyeing him suspiciously.

"That may be the case," the doctor said, "but you're going to have a lot of explaining to do in the morning to a lot of people."

"Damn," O'Grady said, "and I was *leaving* in the morning."

"Sounds like a good idea to me," the doctor said. "By the way, you're not hurt, are you?"

O'Grady took a moment to check. He remembered feeling the tug of a bullet, but it seemed to have passed through the sleeve of his shirt without touching his arm.

"I'm fine."

"That's good news," the sheriff said, coming back around Mark Simmons' horse and pointing his gun at

O'Grady again. "Because you and me are goin' to jail, mister. Let's walk."

"Doc," O'Grady said, "I'd appreciate hearing about Vince Gill's condition—and that of young Simmons, as well."

"Sure," the doctor said. "I'll be over later to let you know."

"Let's go, mister," the sheriff said.

"What's your name, Sheriff?" O'Grady asked.

"Huh? Zeke Harrison. Why?"

"I'm putting you on my list."

The sheriff swallowed and asked, "What list?"

"The list of the most annoying people I've met in my life," O'Grady said. "Come on, let's get to my cell. I could use some sleep."

7

The sun was just coming up when O'Grady opened his eyes. It had been a long time since he'd had to sleep on a hard cot in a jail cell. He'd forgotten how hard it was on your back, even worse than sleeping on the ground.

He stood up and stretched, feeling his muscles loosen. He heard some voices out in the sheriff's office, and then the door opened and the doctor stepped in. He looked as if he hadn't gotten any sleep yet.

"Good morning," the doctor said. He was carrying two cups of coffee, and he handed O'Grady one between the cell bars.

"Thanks," O'Grady said. "*Is* it a good morning?"

"It is for Vince Gill," Doc Fletcher said. "He's going to be fine."

"And the boy?"

"Mark has a broken arm," Fletcher said. "It seems he fell off his horse."

"Fell, hell!" O'Grady said. "I pushed him!"

"I don't know if you want to admit to that," Fletcher said.

"Why not?" O'Grady asked. "It may have broken his arm, but it saved his life."

"Well," Fletcher said, "of course what you say is up to you."

"What's the good sheriff say, this morning?" O'Grady asked.

"He's waiting."

"For what?"

"For Will Purdue and Buck Simmons to come riding in," Fletcher said. "I just hope they don't come riding in at the same time."

"Am I getting caught in between something big?" O'Grady asked.

"Big enough," the doctor said. "Everyone around here knows that Buck Simmons has got two things that Will Purdue wants."

"What are they?"

"His land," Fletcher said, "and his daughter."

"Julia?"

The doctor looked surprised.

"You know Julia?"

"No," O'Grady said, "but I heard about her last night, from Vince Gill. I think he's in love with her, too."

"A lot of men around here are," Fletcher said. "I think it's because she can outride and outshoot most of them."

"Attractive attributes in any woman," O'Grady said, wryly.

"Well, you'll see for yourself when you meet her," Fletcher said.

"Will I?" O'Grady asked. "Be meeting her, I mean?"

"Oh, I think so," Fletcher said. "Her brother's over at the hotel. I wouldn't let him go home tonight. If I know Julia, she'll come looking for him."

"And Gill?"

"Also at the hotel," Fletcher said, "but she won't come looking for him."

"Too bad for Gill," O'Grady said.

"Well," Fletcher said, "I've got to go and get some sleep, Mr. O'Grady."

"Thanks for the coffee, Doc."

"My pleasure," Fletcher said. He turned to face O'Grady again before leaving and said, "I hope you didn't have anyplace urgent to go to."

"I have someplace to go to," O'Grady said. "I won't know whether it's urgent or not until I get there."

"Well, I hope you're not *too* inconvenienced by all of this."

"I guess we'll find out soon enough," O'Grady said, "won't we?"

When Julia Simmons entered the bunkhouse, ranch hands began scrambling for trousers, sheets, blankets, anything to cover themselves up with. Julia, however, was not interested in eyeing their private parts. She stormed across the floor to her uncle's bunk and shook him awake.

"Wha—who—hey!" Bo Simmons shouted. His eyes were open, but he wasn't seeing anything too clearly.

"Uncle Bo!" she shouted. "It's me, Julia!"

"Julia?" Bo rubbed his eyes and then tried to focus on her. "What's wrong, girl?"

"It's Mark, Uncle Bo," she said. "He didn't come home last night."

Bo rubbed a hand over his face and then sat up.

"Wait outside while I get dressed, Julia," he instructed her.

"I'll saddle the horses."

"*My* horse."

"I'm going with you!"

He looked up at her and knew better than to argue with her where her brother was concerned.

"All right," Bo said. "I'll be right out."

Julia went back through the bunkhouse and out, and the men started to dress again.

Off in one corner, Fenner and Colter tried to look as innocent as possible.

Bo Simmons stood up and got dressed, then addressed the entire bunkhouse.

"Who took Mark into town last night?"

Nobody answered.

"I don't have time for this now," he said, his tone menacing, "but whoever you are, you'd better be gone by the time I get back. You're fired."

There was a stunned silence.

"Now," Bo said, "if you don't identify yourselves, you don't get what pay you got coming to you." He walked to the door, then turned and said, "Your choice," before going out

"Some choice," someone said. "Back pay ain't worth havin' to face Bo."

Fenner and Colter looked at each other and silently agreed. They began to pack their belongings.

Will Purdue had gotten in the habit long ago of rising early and walking around his ranch. He liked the idea of having his men see him already up and about when *they* got up in the morning.

As he strolled about the grounds that morning, Larry Rhodes came over to him.

"We got a problem."

"What kind of problem?"

53

"Pete Webber got himself killed last night."

"Where?"

"In town."

"How?"

"Shot."

"Was he alone?"

Rhodes shook his head.

"Bob Owen was with him."

"Dead, too?"

"Yeah."

"He's no loss," Purdue said. "Webber travels in a pack. Who else was with him?"

"Jay Lockheart and Bill Tanner."

"Are they back?"

"Yeah," Rhodes said. "They told me about it this morning."

"You got the whole story?"

"Yep."

"Okay, then," Purdue said. "Fire them, and saddle our horses. We're going into town."

"Right, boss."

"Let them know I don't ever want to see them around here again. Got it?"

"I got it, boss."

"Who killed them?"

"Best I can make out, some stranger. Seems Vince Gill was there, too, though."

"Gill," Purdue said. "He works for Simmons."

"Right?"

Rhodes turned to walk away and Purdue said, "Larry?"

"Yeah, boss?"

"Anything else I should know about?"

"Uh, well . . ."

54

"Larry . . ."

Rhodes turned and looked at his boss.

"Mark Simmons was there."

Purdue's expression hardened.

"Was he hurt?"

"I think so."

"Shot?"

"I don't know."

"Damn . . ." Purdue said. "Okay, don't fire them yet."

"Why not?"

"Because," Purdue said, "if Mark Simmons was seriously hurt, I'm going to take it out of their hides. Get those horses saddled."

When Bo Simmons got to the stable, Julia had her horse and his horse saddled and ready.

"Does your pa know?" Bo asked as they mounted up.

"No," Julia said.

"Okay," Bo said, "we'll check it out and talk to him later."

"Right."

"Let's go, girl. . . ."

8

Sheriff Zeke Harrison was looking out his front window when Bo and Julia Simmons came riding into town. He almost breathed a sigh of relief when he saw them. First, because it wasn't Will Purdue, and second, because it wasn't *Buck* Simmons. Even though Bo was said to be the more dangerous of the two, it was Buck who frightened Zeke Harrison. Then again, anybody with a little money or power or reputation frightened Zeke Harrison.

He took a deep breath, opened his office door, and stepped out. He watched as Julia Simmons and her uncle rode past him. They'd check on Mark first, get the story from him and the doctor, and then they'd come back to him.

Harrison turned and went back inside.

"It's starting!" he shouted out to O'Grady.

"What is?" O'Grady called back.

"Mark Simmons' sister and uncle just rode into town," Harrison said.

"Good," O'Grady said. "The sooner we get this cleared up, the better."

Harrison went into the back so he could look at O'Grady when he talked to him.

"You should have found out who you were dealing with before you started trouble, stranger."

"What the hell kind of lawman are you, anyway?" O'Grady demanded.

"Whataya mean?"

"You haven't even talked to anybody, witnesses, anybody who saw what happened last night, and already you're blaming me for what happened."

"It don't matter who started it, friend," Harrison said. "Both Will Purdue and Buck Simmons are involved. They're powerful people around here."

"Powerful to you, maybe," O'Grady said. "I can see they scare you plenty, but they don't mean shot to me . . . *friend*."

Harrison's eyes widened. He wondered if he could ever talk that way about Will Purdue. He wished he could.

Scared? Sure he was scared, and the only reason the stranger wasn't was *because* he was a stranger.

"I got work to do," he mumbled, and backed away from the stranger's accusing glare.

As the sheriff left the room, O'Grady sat down on his cot. He wasn't about to fold just because he'd happened to get himself involved in a problem between two local ranchers, no matter *how* powerful they were around here. All he had to do was get to a telegraph and he'd show them some *real* power.

No, he scolded himself immediately, *I can't do that*. The United States government was not involved in this. This was a personal matter, and he was going to have to handle it that way.

He wondered idly if he'd make it to Hastings in time.

*   *   *

57

Julia and Bo Simmons entered Dr. Aaron Fletcher's office. Fletcher, who had gotten only a few hours' sleep, looked up at them with red-rimmed eyes.

"What happened, Doc?" Fletcher asked.

"The sheriff can tell you that better than I can," Fletcher said.

"I doubt that," Bo Simmons said. He had no use for the sheriff of Eli's Crossing. The man was weak.

"Well, Vince Gill, then."

"Vince, maybe," Bo said, "but I want to hear it from you first. We heard as soon as we rode in that something happened to Mark last night."

"People were dying to tell us," Julia added.

"People generally like to give other people bad news," Fletcher said. "It's better than getting bad news themselves, I guess."

"In two years' time," Julia said, "Will Purdue has gotten this town behind him, somehow."

"He's a charming man," Fletcher said.

"Not from where I'm standing," Julia said, making a face.

"How bad is the boy hurt?" Bo asked, interrupting their conversation about Purdue.

"He's got a broken arm, Bo," Fletcher said, "that's all."

Julia breathed a sigh of relief. Bo felt her relax next to him.

"How did it happen?"

"There was a shooting," Fletcher said. "Some boys from the Purdue ranch were after a stranger. Gill was there. Mark was on his horse, drunk. Apparently two of *your* boys brought him to town, got him drunk, and left him."

"And?" Julia asked.

"When the shooting started, Mark was on his horse. The stranger pushed him off to get him out of the line of fire. He broke his arm when he fell."

Julia and Bo exchanged a glance, and then Bo asked, "What about Gill?"

"Took a bullet in the hip. He'll be off his feet for a while."

"Where is he?"

"At the hotel," Fletcher said. "So is Mark."

"Can they go back to the ranch?"

"You can take Mark back today," Fletcher said. "Give Gill another day before you try to move him."

"All right," Bo said. "What about the other men? They were from Purdue's bunch?"

"Yes," Fletcher said. "Pete Webber, and one other. There were two more, but apparently they ran off."

"Do you know what started it?" Bo asked.

"That I don't know," the doctor said. "You'll *have* to talk to the sheriff about that."

"No, I won't," Bo said. "I bet *he* don't know what started it. We can't move Gill, but can I talk to him?"

"Sure."

Bo looked at Julia and said, "Let's go over to the hotel. You check on Mark, and I'll talk to Gill. In fact, you can stay with Mark while I go over to the jail and talk to the stranger."

"I want to come, too," she said.

Bo gave Fletcher a look of frustration, then said to Julia, "All right, all right. Jeez, the woman won't let me do a thing without her."

She smiled and kissed her uncle on the cheek.

"You wouldn't have it any other way."

Julia and Bo walked over to the hotel, obtained the

room numbers they needed from the clerk, and both went upstairs.

Bo entered Gill's room, and the man opened his eyes and looked at him.

"Hello, Bo," Gill said.

"How're you doin', Vince?"

"I'm fine," Gill said. He tried to move and grimaced in pain. "Be back at work in no time."

"No you won't," Bo said. "You take it easy until you're healed."

"I'm a fast healer," Gill said. "When can I go back to the ranch?"

"We'll bring a buckboard in for you tomorrow."

"And Mark?"

"Julia and I will take him back today."

"Julia's here?"

Bo nodded.

"She's in with Mark."

"Oh . . ." Gill's disappointment was obvious, but Bo ignored it. He didn't have time for that.

"Gill, tell me what happened."

Gill explain the situation to Bo, starting with what had happened in the saloon, and how it had extended out into the street later on.

"Now tell me about Mark."

Again, he gave Bo the whole story about Fenner and Colter getting Mark drunk.

"O'Grady was helping me get him on his horse when Webber and the others started shooting. If O'Grady hadn't shoved Mark out of the saddle the boy might have gotten shot. As it is, he's lucky he only got a broken arm."

"He wouldn't have gotten that if he wasn't drunk," Bo observed.

"That's right."

"Well, Fenner and Colter better be cleared out by the time I get back to the ranch, if they know what's good for them."

"Bo, about O'Grady," Gill said. "I think he's in jail. We should get him out."

"We will, don't worry," Bo said. He put his hand on Gill's shoulder and said, "I appreciate what you did for Mark last night."

"I was just trying to bring him home safe."

"Well, that means a lot, Vince," Bo said. "I'll see you tomorrow, all right?"

"Sure, Bo," Gill said. "Uh, about Julia . . ."

"Yeah?"

Gill hesitated, then said, "No, never mind. I'll see you tomorrow."

Bo nodded and stepped out into the hall. At the same time—as if by some sixth sense—Julia came out of Mark's room.

"How's the boy?" he asked.

"He doesn't remember much."

"He remember Colter and Fenner?"

"Yes," she said. "He says he came to town with them, but doesn't know what happened to them."

"Nothing happened to them," Bo said, then added with feeling, "and nothing will, as long as they're gone by the time we get back."

Julia gave her uncle a puzzled look.

"Come on," he said, without explaining, "let's go over to the jail and talk to this stranger."

9

Sheriff Zeke Harrison saw Julia and Bo Simmons step out of the hotel and start down the street toward his office. He hurried back inside, so that he would be seated behind his desk when they came in.

As they entered, Bo Simmons came in first and then Julia followed, closing the door behind her.

"Bo," Harrison said. "Miss Simmons."

"Never mind the pleasantries, Zeke," Bo said gruffly. "I want to know what happened last night."

"Well," the sheriff said, "we got this stranger in town who started some trouble."

"Bullshit!" Bo said. "Don't feed me shit, Zeke. I want to talk to the man and hear from him what happened."

"You'd believe him over me?" Zeke Harrison asked.

"You bet," Bo Simmons said. "I want to talk to him—*now*."

"Okay," Harrison said, "all right, I'll take you back there."

"I know the way, Zeke," Bo said. "I've bailed enough of our boys out of here. Come on, Julia."

"Hey, she can't go back there!"

"Just sit tight and keep your mouth shut, Zeke,"

Julia said to him before her uncle could speak. "You'll be a lot happier that way."

Zeke Harrison stared at her, not believing what she had said. She sure was more like her uncle than her father.

O'Grady looked up when he heard the door to the cell block open and saw two people enter, a man and a woman. From the descriptions he had heard, he knew that the woman was Julia Simmons.

"Miss Simmons," he said, standing up.

Julia Simmons seemed about to speak and then stopped short, staring at him. Bo looked at Julia, wondering what was wrong with her.

"I'm Bo Simmons, mister," the man said.

"I'm Canyon O'Grady. Are you a relation to Buck Simmons? And Mark?"

"That's right," Bo said. "Buck's brother and Mark—and Julia's—uncle."

"How is Mark?" O'Grady asked.

"The boy's all right," Bo said. He reached up with one hand to take hold of one of the bars, and leaned forward. "He's got a broken arm, but he's gonna be fine. I understand we got you to thank for that."

"For the broken arm," O'Grady asked, "or for him being fine?"

"Well . . . both, I reckon. Uh, listen, you want to tell us what happened last night, from start to finish? We been gettin' bits and pieces."

"Sure," O'Grady said, and related the whole story from the moment he'd entered town until the time he shot Pete Webber.

Bo looked at Julia, who still hadn't spoken up to that point.

"What do you say, Julia?" Bo asked his niece. "Should we get this fella out of jail?"

"I think so, Uncle Bo," she said, looking at her uncle. "I believe him."

"Yeah," Bo said. "Yessir, I believe him, too."

"Can you get me out?" O'Grady asked.

"I think so, Mr. O'Grady," Bo said. "Course, my brother will want you to come out to the ranch so's he can thank you in person."

"And for dinner," Julia added.

"Well," O'Grady said, "I *was* planning on leaving early this morning, but I guess that's out of the question. Sure, if you can get me out, I'd be glad to come out to the ranch for dinner."

"All right," Bo said, slapping one hand against the bars. "I'll talk to the sheriff. Julia, why don't you keep this young fella company back here while I do that?"

"Sure, Uncle Bo," Julia said.

Bo left them alone, and Julia Simmons looked a bit uncomfortable.

"I've heard a lot about you," O'Grady started.

"Oh, really?" she asked. "Was any of it good?"

"It was all good," O'Grady said.

"Who's been talking about me?"

"Vince Gill," O'Grady said. "He's . . . impressed by you."

"Is he?" she asked. "Well, I've known Vince for a long time. I think he's a little prejudiced."

"Well then," O'Grady said, "I guess I'll just have to form my own opinions then, won't I?"

Julia stared at him and then said, "I suppose you will."

They were staring at each other when they both

became aware of raised voices from the sheriff's office.

"I'll be back," Julia said.

She hurried from the cell block in time to see her uncle facing off with Larry Rhodes, the foreman of the Purdue spread. Will Purdue himself was standing behind Rhodes, and just to the right.

". . . wasn't talkin' to you, Rhodes, I was talkin' to your boss," Bo Simmons was saying.

"Never mind who you was talkin' to, Bo," Larry Rhodes said, "I'm talkin' to *you* now."

"Sheriff," Purdue said, "I want that man held here until the judge gets back."

"The judge won't be back 'til next week, Mr. Purdue," Sheriff Harrison said.

"That's fine with me," Purdue said, but Bo cut him off.

"Zeke," he said, whirling on the lawman, "I want you to let that man out of that cell right now!"

"Don't do it, Zeke," Purdue said.

Harrison looked back and forth between the two men, despair plain on his face.

"Bo," Julia said, stepping between her uncle and Rhodes. "Step back, Larry."

Rhodes blinked and then took a step away from her.

"Let me talk to Will," she said to her uncle.

"Julia . . ."

"Just step into the back with Mr. O'Grady, Bo," she said. "Will and I want to talk."

"Larry," Purdue said, "wait outside."

Rhodes looked at Purdue, then back at Bo. Each man seemed to be waiting for the other to leave the room first. Finally, Bo stepped into the cell block, and Larry Rhodes stepped outside.

"Sheriff?" Julia said.

"Yeah?"

"Get out."

Harrison blinked this time, then looked at Will Purdue, who was staring hard at him.

" 'Get out,' " the sheriff repeated as he walked to the door. "Gettin' thrown out of my own office!"

"What's going on out there?" O'Grady asked Bo Simmons.

"I don't know," Bo said, looking at O'Grady. "I got kicked out by my niece. She's talking to Will Purdue right now."

"The men I killed worked for Purdue, didn't they?" O'Grady asked.

"That's right," Bo said. "He wants you held until our judge comes back next week."

"I can't stay here until next week."

"Julia's talkin' to Purdue right now," Bo said. "She'll get you out."

"Maybe," O'Grady said, "but at what cost?"

"Huh?"

"What is she going to give him for my freedom?" O'Grady asked.

"I don't know. . . ." Bo said, frowning.

"Go and tell her not to do it."

"Mr. O'Grady," Bo said, "you don't know my niece. Tell her not to do somethin', and that's the way to get her to do it."

"Well, what is?"

Bo looked at O'Grady and said, "I can't figure her

out any more than I could her mother. We'll just have to see what she has up her sleeve."

"What are you going to offer me, Julia?" Will Purdue asked, folding his arms.

"Nothing, Will," she said. "I'm not offering you anything. I'm just telling you that I want that man out of jail . . . today."

Purdue's expression said that he was confused, and amazed at the same time.

"Why would I do that?"

"Well, for one thing, witnesses will say that your men started the trouble," she said.

"Is that so?"

"Yes, that's so," she said. "Witnesses inside the saloon and out on the street will say that your man Webber started all the trouble."

"Julia, I—"

"My *brother* was out there, Will!" she said, cutting him off. "That man saved my brother's life. I will not let him stay in that cell."

"Very well, then," Purdue said, "make me an offer."

"Will Purdue," she said, "you disgust me."

"You know you don't mean that, Julia," Purdue said.

"You're arrogant!"

"Well, *that's* true," he said. "Look, I'll make *you* an offer, okay?"

She folded her arms now and glared at him. After a moment she spoke.

"All right," she said, "make it."

"Let me escort you to the party tonight."

"What party?"

"You know, the engagement party? You'll need an escort, you know."

She stared at him.

"That's all you want?" she said.

He spread his arms and inquired innocently, "What did you expect me to ask for?"

"I don't know," she said. "More than that."

"Well, that's all I want, and I'll support you in getting the sheriff to let the man out of jail."

Julia thought it over for fully two minutes while Purdue waited patiently.

"All right, Will," she said. "I'll go to the party with you, but that doesn't mean I'll leave with you. Is that understood?"

"Perfectly, Julia," he said. "I agree to those terms."

"All right, then," she said, "tell the sheriff to let him out."

"I'll take care of it."

"I'll go and tell Mr. O'Grady and Bo."

"And I'll see you tonight, Julia," Will said. "I'll come to your ranch to get you."

"If you do that," she said, "my father will kill you. I'll come to your ranch."

"As you wish," Purdue said. "See you tonight, Julia dear."

She closed her eyes and, with her back to him, made a face. She *hated* it when he called her "dear."

She returned to O'Grady's cell and told him, "You're free to go. The sheriff will be here in a moment to let you out."

"What'd you say to Purdue?" Bo demanded.

"I said I wanted Mr. O'Grady out."

"And he agreed?"

"Yes."

"Why?"

"Uncle Bo . . ." she said. The comment was meant to put her uncle off, but Bo would not be put off.

"Come on, girl," he said. "Will Purdue ain't just gonna roll over like that for no reason."

"What do you think I gave him?" she demanded.

"I'd kind of like to know the answer to that question myself," O'Grady said.

Julia switched her gaze from her uncle to Canyon O'Grady.

"Why?"

He shrugged.

"I'd kind of like to know what I'm worth."

"Not a lot," she said, shortly.

"Oh."

"Julia, I—" Bo started.

"All right, Uncle Bo," she cut in. "I agreed to go to the party with him tonight."

"The engagement party?"

"That's right," she said, lifting her chin. "I have to go anyway, so I might as well have an escort."

"Oh, sure," Bo said. "You're going to walk in on Will Purdue's arm. How do you think *that's* gonna look?"

"I don't know how it's going to look," she said. "We'll find out tonight."

"What's your pa gonna say?" Bo asked.

"Nothing," she said, "because we're not going to tell him. Understand?"

"Julia . . ." Bo said, warningly.

"Uncle Bo," she said, "you *have* to do this for me . . . please?"

O'Grady saw plainly that Bo Simmons could not deny his niece anything.

"All right, girl, all right."

"And you?" Julia said to O'Grady.

"Me?"

"Not a word."

"*I'm* not going to tell anyone," he said. "I want to get out of here, remember?"

At that moment Sheriff Zeke Harrison walked in, looking totally confused. He unlocked O'Grady's cell and said, "You're free to go."

"Thank you, Sheriff."

"I have your gun belt out by my desk."

Harrison left. O'Grady retrieved his hat and stepped out of the cell, only to be confronted by a stern-looking Julia Simmons.

"Remember," she said, "not a *word* to my father."

"Of course not," O'Grady said. "You're going to tell him yourself, aren't you?"

Julia took a step back, away from the question.

"Ain't you?" Bo asked.

She looked at both men in turn, then said, "Probably," and walked out.

10

By the time O'Grady had picked up his gun belt from the desk, reloaded his weapon and strapped it on, and then stepped outside, Bo and Julia Simmons were nose-to-nose again.

"I don't want to argue about it, Uncle Bo," Julia said. "What's done is done."

"Well, maybe you ain't gonna tell your father," Bo said, "but he's sure as hell gonna know when he gets to that party."

"What party do we keep talking about?" O'Grady asked.

"What time is it?" Bo asked, rubbing his hand over his mouth. "Is the saloon open yet? You care for a drink, Mr. O'Grady?"

"Well," O'Grady said, "to tell you the truth I'd kind of like to have breakfast before I start drinking."

"With Uncle Bo," Julia said, "drinking *is* breakfast."

"That ain't true, Julia," Bo said. "I like breakfast just fine."

"Could I *buy* the two of you breakfast?" O'Grady asked. "I mean, as my way of saying thanks?"

"Well, not for me," Bo said, "but I tell you what. You can buy Julia breakfast while I go and arrange for a buckboard to take Mark home in."

"I can help you with—" Julia started to say, but her uncle wouldn't hear of it.

"I don't need help getting a buckboard, Julia," he said, "but Mr. O'Grady here, he might just need help finding someplace good to have breakfast."

"I *could* use a good breakfast," O'Grady said to Julia, "and some company to eat it with."

"Well . . . all right, then," Julia said. "We'll go to Ma's."

"Your mother's?"

"No," she said, "not *my* mother's. Just a place to eat, and everyone calls the woman who cooks 'Ma.' "

"Oh," O'Grady said. "So then she isn't really any-one's mother?"

"I'm gonna get goin'," Bo said, and slipped away.

"Well," Julia said, leading O'Grady in the other direction, "I'm sure she *is* someone's mother—or *was* at some point."

Ma's turned out to have excellent food, but O'Grady found himself more interested in his dining partner than in the food.

He could see what Vince Gill had been talking about. Julia Simmons was not a classic beauty by any means, but there was something about her that constantly drew your eyes to her. She was tall and slender for the most part, except for her full breasts, which her clothing—*men's* clothing—did nothing to hide. Her brown hair was cut short, probably so it wouldn't get in her way while she was working. She had wide-set brown eyes, a strong jawline and chin, and a full mouth. Her mannerisms, while certainly not *manly,* were nevertheless hardly feminine.

O'Grady noticed that her hands were work-worn, yet still managed to look graceful.

She caught him looking at her hands and drew them back into her lap.

"What's wrong?"

"Nothing."

"You were staring at my hands."

"No I wasn't."

"Yes you were."

"Well . . . they're very nice hands."

Now she was self-conscious, but she couldn't finish eating with her hands in her lap, so she finally took them out again.

"Did you meet my brother at all last night?" she asked, changing the subject.

"Yes I did, briefly," O'Grady said. "He came in with the other two men—Fenner and Colter?—and Gill called him over to introduce me. Uh, Gill was trying to find out if I was interested in a job. He's the foreman out there, is he?"

"No," she said, "my Uncle Bo is the foreman, but Vince has been with my father for a long time. Sometimes he'll bring someone in to work. He's a good judge of people, usually."

"Meaning, not in this case?"

"Oh, no," she said hurriedly. "I didn't mean that at all."

"It's okay," he said, "I was just teasing."

"Oh . . ."

"Trying to get you to smile," he went on. "You do smile, don't you?"

"Well, of course," she said, without smiling. "Everyone smiles . . . sometime."

"What about you?"

She heaved a big sigh and said, "I just don't seem to have the time, lately."

"Things are rough now, huh?"

"Well . . . we have fallen on some hard times, but we could get through them if there wasn't so much . . . pressure."

"Pressure from who?"

"Well, the bank, for one thing," she said. "And we *know* that Purdue is behind that."

"Purdue has a lot of power around here, doesn't he?" he asked.

"Yes," she said, "and he's gotten it in a short period of time. I mean, my father has been here for fifteen years. Will Purdue came in two years ago with his *money*, and he's got most of the town on his side, now."

"Money can do that to people."

"Money . . ." she said, shaking her head.

"Does he think his money can buy you?"

"He thinks it can buy anyone," she said. "He was shocked when my father turned down his offers to buy the ranch. Now he's got all of these gunmen working for him. It's as if he thinks he can *scare* us into selling."

"And he can't?"

She put down her fork and stared across the table at him.

"My mother *died* trying to help my father build our place up," she said, with feeling. "You don't just *sell* that!"

"No," he said, "you sure don't."

She realized then the harshness of her tone, and sat back.

"I'm sorry," she said, "I didn't mean to take it out

74

on you. It's just that Will Purdue makes me . . . so goddamned *angry!*"

O'Grady studied her for a moment, then decided to go ahead and say what he was thinking.

"You liked him once, didn't you?"

She looked at him quickly, looked away, then firmed her chin and looked back.

"Yes," she said. "When he first came he was very charming and we were . . . seeing each other for a while. Then when he showed his true colors I wanted nothing more to do with him."

"But he won't take no for an answer, right?"

"Right," she said. "But that's the only answer he's going to keep getting."

"Except for tonight, huh?"

She looked away.

"I appreciate what it must have taken for you to do that . . . for me."

She looked at him and said, "You saved my brother's life, Mr. O'Grady. We don't take that kind of thing very lightly."

"Well," he said, "if I saved your brother's life, the least you could do is call me Canyon."

"All right . . . Canyon."

"We should check on your uncle," he said. "I can help get your brother into the buckboard, then I'm going to take a bath and wash off this jail smell."

"You smell fine," she said, then looked away in embarrassment.

75

11

When O'Grady was reintroduced to Mark Simmons, the young man said he remembered him.

"I don't remember much else that happened after that, though," he also admitted.

"You *know* you shouldn't drink," Julia said, chucking her brother lightly behind the head.

Mark Simmons gave his sister an irritated look, but it quickly faded. O'Grady thought by looking at them that Julia and Mark loved each other very much.

As it turned out, they really didn't need much help getting Mark into the buckboard. He was able to walk down the stairs with Bo on one side and Julia on the other. O'Grady simply walked ahead.

"I understand I have you to thank for this," Mark said, indicating his arm, "and also for me not getting shot. Thanks."

"My pleasure," O'Grady said. "I just wish there had been a gentler way for me to do it, at the time."

"I'll take a broken arm over a bullet, any day," Mark said. "Besides, this will keep me away from hard work for a while."

"Maybe Pa will teach you the paperwork involved in running a ranch," Julia said.

Mark looked pained and said, "Oh no, paperwork?

Bo, can you find something for me to do one-handed?"

"We'll find you something, boy," Bo said. "Don't you worry none."

"Care to ride out with us now, Mr.—I mean, Canyon?" Julia asked O'Grady.

"No thanks, Julia," he said. "I really do need that bath."

"Well, come out later then," she said. "About five, before the party."

"You don't have to worry about giving me dinner if you have a party to go to."

"Don't be silly," she said. "You'll come to the party, too. You can eat there."

"I don't have any party clothes," he noted.

"Go over to the haberdasher's and buy something," she said, mounting her horse. "Tell him to put it on our bill. We'll see you about six?"

He nodded and said, "Six it is."

He watched as they rode away. Bo had tied his horse to the back of the buckboard he was driving, and Julia rode alongside. She rode tall and proud in the saddle, with her back straight.

O'Grady was impressed with Julia Simmons.

From the front window of the bank, Will Purdue watched as the Simmonses rode out of town. After they were gone he stared at Canyon O'Grady until the tall, red-haired man had gone back into the hotel.

"Boss?"

He turned at the sound of Larry Rhodes' voice.

"What?"

"We got to get back to the ranch, boss," Rhodes said. "There ain't much we can do here."

"In a little while," Purdue said.

"Is there somethin' you wanna do, boss?"

"Yes," Purdue said, "I want to find out as much about that man O'Grady as I can."

"How you gonna do that?"

"By telegraph, Larry," Purdue said. He turned to his foreman and said, "You can go back to the ranch. I'll be along soon."

"I'd just as soon stay with you, if you don't mind," Rhodes said. He saw himself not just as Will Purdue's foreman, but as his bodyguard as well. Most of the townspeople accepted the fact that the influx of Will Purdue's money was the reason their own was growing, but men like Purdue always managed to make enemies.

"Watching my back, Larry?"

"That's what I get paid for, boss."

"Actually," Purdue said, putting his hand on Rhodes' shoulder, "it's not, but I appreciate it, anyway. Come on. Let's go over to the telegraph office."

From his hotel window, O'Grady saw Will Purdue and his foreman walk down the street from the bank to the telegraph office. Well, if he were Will Purdue he'd check up on the stranger in town, as well. It made sense that the man wanted to try to find out who he was going up against.

Not that O'Grady intended to go up against the wealthy rancher. He'd go out to this party with the Simmonses, then leave town early in the morning. He still had time to make it to Hastings at that appointed time.

Unless something else happened, of course.

*　　*　　*

After his bath, O'Grady dressed in fresh clothes for the second time since arriving, then decided to get his other clothes washed before he left town.

He stopped at the front desk to ask the clerk if there was a laundry in town.

"Yes, sir," the man said. "Down the block to the left, and around the corner. It's a Chinese laundry, sir."

"What a surprise," O'Grady said.

"Sir?"

"Never mind," O'Grady said. "Thank you."

He left the hotel and walked his dirty clothes around the corner to the Chinese laundry.

"You want wash?" the Chinaman behind the counter asked with a big yellow, gap-toothed smile.

"I want wash," O'Grady said.

In the back of the laundry he saw a young and pretty Chinese woman working on some clothes. She looked up at him once, caught his eyes and held them briefly, then looked away. Her incredibly long hair was hanging down over her shoulders, and he wondered how she could work without it getting in her way.

"You come back tomorrow," the Chinaman said. "Tomorrow."

"No, no," O'Grady said. "I need them back today, this afternoon."

"Yes," the Chinaman said, nodding his head, "tomorrow. You come back tomorrow."

"No," O'Grady said, "no—" He suddenly realized he was wasting his time, the man didn't understand him. "Excuse me?" he called to the young woman in the back.

She looked up at him and he beckoned to her. She wiped her hands and came out to see what he wanted.

"I'm sorry, this man . . ."

"My father," she said.

"Yes, your father, he doesn't seem to understand what I'm saying."

"He does not understand English."

"Can *you* help me, then?" O'Grady asked. "I need these clothes back this afternoon. Is that possible?"

"Yes," she said, "I will take care of it. You come back this afternoon."

"Yes," the Chinaman said, "tomorrow."

She smiled then, and became not just pretty but beautiful.

"They will be ready this afternoon," she assured him.

"Thank you. What's your name?"

"Li."

"Thank you, Li. I am Canyon."

"Canyon," she said, and nodded.

"Canyon," the old man said.

O'Grady smiled at both of them and said, "See you later."

"Yes," the Chinaman said, "tomorrow."

12

Will Purdue was frustrated. All of the people he had sent telegraph messages to had responded as he'd wanted them to, quickly. However, they had all responded in the negative.

"This can't be," he told Larry Rhodes.

They were in the saloon, sitting at a table with a beer in front of each of them. It was still early, and there were only three other people in the place, including the bartender.

"Nobody has ever heard of this man?" he said.

"Why should they, boss?" Rhodes said. "What if he's just . . . nobody?"

"He killed two of my men, Larry," Purdue said. "That makes him somebody to me."

"Well then, look at it this way," Rhodes said. "When you let me take care of him, nobody is gonna miss him."

"Yes," Purdue said, running the thumbnail of his right hand over his bottom lip, "that is one way to look at it."

"Then I can take care of him?"

"No," Purdue said, thoughtfully, "not yet."

"Boss . . ."

"I'll tell you when, Larry," Purdue said.

"Okay," Rhodes said, "you're the boss."

"Finish your beer," Purdue said. "We're heading back to the ranch."

O'Grady was sitting in a straight-backed wooden chair in front of the hotel when Purdue and his foreman came out of the saloon. He had seen the man walk back and forth between the saloon—which had been opened for Purdue—and the telegraph office, and had wondered idly if Purdue owned a piece of the saloon.

O'Grady was fairly sure that Purdue would find out nothing from all his telegraph messages—that is, unless the man had a contact high up in the government. From the unhappy look on the faces of both men, he assumed that was not the case.

So, the wealthy rancher hadn't been able to satisfy his curiosity about Canyon O'Grady. It would be interesting to see what his next step would be. Whatever it was, O'Grady figured he'd better make it quick, because by morning he intended to be gone.

O'Grady's intention was to head for the Simmons ranch at five P.M. At three he went back to the Chinese laundry to retrieve his clothes. When he got there he saw two men in the place ahead of him, only they didn't seem to be bringing in any clothes, or picking up any. They only seemed intent on causing trouble.

The old man was talking in rapid-fire Chinese, waving his arms wildly and pointing at the door. O'Grady assumed that the man was telling them to get out. His daughter was standing behind him. It was to the man's pretty daughter that the two men were talking. They were making lewd remarks and suggestions to her, and she looked very frightened.

O'Grady first impulse was to back away and mind his own business, but the daughter saw him over the shoulder of one of the men, and the pleading in her eyes was almost like a shout for help.

It was a shout Canyon O'Grady could not bring himself to ignore.

He stepped into the store.

"Scuse me, fellas," he said, sliding between the two men. They moved to accommodate him, and one of them ended up a little off-balance. "Are my clothes ready?" Canyon asked the old man.

"Hey," the first man said to O'Grady, "watch who you're pushin'!"

"Sorry," O'Grady said, looking at both men in turn, "just trying to pick up my laundry."

"Yeah, well, we were here first."

"No tickee! No tickee!" the old Chinaman was shouting at O'Grady, while pointing to the other men.

"The man says you have no ticket," O'Grady said.

"Oh, is that what he's sayin'?" one of the two men said, laughing. "We ain't got no tickee because we didn't bring in no clothes."

O'Grady looked at their hands and said, "I don't see that you're bringing in any clothes, either."

"That's right," the second man said, "we ain't."

"Then I guess you don't have any business here," O'Grady concluded.

"Not *laundry* business," the second man said, laughing, "but we got other business."

"With her," the first man said, pointing to the old man's daughter.

"She's got work to do," O'Grady said.

"Hey," the first man said, "all we wanna do is take her on a little picnic!"

"You want to go on a picnic with these men?" O'Grady asked Li.

She shook her head, her eyes wide.

"She says no."

"Well," the second man said, "we say yes."

Annoyed now, O'Grady turned to face both men.

"Look, I'm trying to collect my clothes here. The girl has already said she's not interested. Why don't you fellas just get lost?"

"Get *lost*?" the first man said, widening his eyes. He looked at his friend and said, "Did you hear that? This fella wants us to get lost."

"I heard," the second man said. He looked at O'Grady and said, "That ain't nice, mister."

O'Grady knew what was going to happen. They'd go 'round and 'round a few more times, then the two men would either try to pound him or go for their guns. They were both wearing well-worn rigs that looked like they'd seen a lot of use. O'Grady decided he might as well move first and get it over with.

"I think it's time you boys left," he said.

"Oh yeah?" one of them said. "Well, what if we ain't ready to—"

He didn't allow the man to finish what he was saying. He placed one hand against each man's chest and pushed with all his might.

One man staggered back, out the door and sprawling into the street. The other man didn't make the doorway. He struck the doorjamb hard, grunting from the impact. O'Grady followed him, removed his gun from his holster, spun him around, and shoved him out the door.

He went flying into the street just as the other man was trying to get up. They both went down in a tangled heap. O'Grady tucked the extra gun into his belt and turned to go back to the counter.

"Are my clothes ready?" he asked Li.

"Yes," she said, nodding. "They are ready."

He waited while she went into the back.

The old man pointed out the door and said, "No tickee!"

"I know, old man," O'Grady said. "No tickee."

Li came back out and handed him a package wrapped in brown paper and tied.

"How much do I owe you?"

"No charge," she said.

O'Grady put two dollars down on the counter, anyway.

"Thank you," she said to him, and it wasn't for the two dollars.

"You're welcome."

As he headed for the door she called out, "You be careful!"

"Of what?" he asked over his shoulder.

"Those men," she said. "They work for Mr. Purdue."

He stopped short and turned to look at her.

"*Will* Purdue?"

She nodded.

He closed his eyes, shook his head, said, "Just great," and stepped out into the street.

13

As O'Grady stepped outside, the two men in the street glared at him. The one whose gun he had taken shouted.

"Hey! You got my gun!"

O'Grady looked at him.

"If I give it back to you, you're only going to get hurt."

He started to walk away and the man called, "Hey! Hey, my gun! Zack!" He was speaking to the other man. "Don't let him walk away! Zack! Draw your gun!"

Apparently, however, Zack was not so eager to take on O'Grady—or anyone—alone.

"Zack, you coward!"

"Oh yeah?" Zack shouted back. "Why don't you go and get your rifle, if you're so brave? Your horse is right over there!"

"He's got my gun!" the other man shouted, as if he were looking for somebody—anybody—to help him.

While the two men argued, O'Grady quickened his pace, turned the corner, and headed back to the hotel, his laundry underneath his left arm. He left his right arm free just in case the man *did* grab his rifle.

O'Grady marveled at the coincidence of running

into more of Will Purdue's men. It was as if fate were decreeing that he and Purdue should cross swords. He was going to head fate off, though, by leaving town early the next morning. He would have left tonight, but he'd promised Julia Simmons that he would come out to her father's ranch.

Canyon O'Grady never broke a promise to a lady, if he could help it.

Out at the Simmons ranch, Buck Simmons had the sneaking suspicion that something was going on that he didn't know about.

He had tried to talk to Mark, who'd only said, "My arm hurts, Pa. I'm gonna go lie down."

He had tried to talk to Bo, who had said, "I got to go out and check that fence in the east pasture, Buck. We can talk when I get back."

Finally he cornered Julia in the kitchen, where she couldn't get away, and asked *her* what was going on.

"What do you mean, Pa?"

"Everybody's avoiding me, Julia," Buck said. "Do I have the plague, or something?"

"Of course not, Papa," she said.

"Uh-oh."

"What does *that* mean?" Julia asked.

He narrowed his eyes.

"Whenever you call me 'Papa' you're hiding something," he said.

She gaped at him and said, "That's silly."

"Silly or not, it's been that way ever since you were a little girl. Whenever you're lying to me, or there's something you don't want to tell me, you call me 'Papa.' Now what's going on, Julia?"

"Nothing . . ."

"Julia!"

"Well . . . we're having a guest tonight."

"What guest?"

"Canyon O'Grady."

"What's a Canyon O'Grady?"

"You remember," she said. "I told you, he's the man who saved Mark's life."

"Oh yeah, him," Buck said. "Why's he coming out here?"

"So you can thank him, Pap—uh, Pa," she said, looking away.

"Does he know that we're all going to a party tonight?' Buck asked. "Or did *you* forget."

"Of course I didn't forget my best friend's engagement party, Pa," Julia said. "No, I told him that he could come with us."

"What?"

"Don't worry, Pa," Julia said. "Nobody will mind. In fact, I'll be leaving . . . a little earlier than everyone else."

"Why is that?"

"Well . . . Theresa wants all of her bridesmaids to come a little early."

"I thought you were her maid of honor," Buck said.

She made a face at him and said, "Same thing, Pa."

"Oh," he said, frowning. "I don't know, but I get the feeling something *else* is going on that I don't know anything about."

"Well, maybe you should ask Mark or Bo about it, then," she suggested.

"I would," he mumbled, turning to leave the kitchen, "if I could get either one of them to give me the time of day."

As he left the kitchen, Julia put her hands down

flat on the table and heaved a sigh of relief. She knew that all she had done was put off the inevitable, but that was what she had *wanted* to do. She didn't want to have to tell her father what she had done until it was absolutely necessary. And from now on she was going to have to watch that business of calling him "Papa." . . .

"You let him take your gun?" Will Purdue asked in disbelief, as he faced the two men from behind his desk.

Billy Pitt hung his head down and said, "It happened so fast."

"Yeah," said Zack Lutz.

"And *your* gun?" Purdue asked.

"No, sir," Lutz said, "I still got mine."

"That's 'cause you was too scared to draw it," Pitt mumbled.

"Why should I get shot trying to get back your gun?" Lutz demanded, turning to face Pitt and sticking his jaw out.

"Enough," Purdue said.

He looked at Larry Rhodes, who shrugged. The two men had returned from town and had told Rhodes what happened. Rhodes had taken them to Purdue.

"Tell me what happened," Purdue said.

"Well, we wasn't doin' nothin', really."

Purdue stood up and was around the desk faster than any of the other three men could follow. He slapped Billy Pitt open-handed across the face, rocking the man's head back and splitting his lip.

"I'll ask you again to tell me what happened in town," Purdue said, "and you better not lie to me, Billy! Understand?"

"Sure, boss," Billy said, licking the blood from his lip, "I understand."

"Now go ahead. . . ."

Billy looked at Lutz, who looked away, and then said, "Well, we were trying to get this little Chinese gal to . . ."

When he had heard all of Pitt's story, Purdue told Rhodes to get the two men out of his sight.

Rhodes walked the two men out and then came back.

"First he kills two of my men," Purdue said, "then he disarms one and makes the other one too frightened to act."

"What are you thinking, boss?"

"I'm thinking that maybe Buck Simmons is finally bringing in some professional help."

"One man?"

"It's all he's needed so far, isn't it?"

"Boss, if I send four or five men against him, that will be the end of it."

"No, not yet," Purdue said. "I want to find out for sure if he's working for the Simmonses."

"How you gonna do that?"

"Not how," Purdue said. "Where."

"Okay, where?"

"At the party tonight that old man Watson is throwing for his daughter," Purdue said. "We should be able to see what's going on there."

"If he shows up."

"That's right," Purdue said.

"And what if he just leaves town?"

"Then he won't be a problem."

"But . . . he killed two of our men! We can't just let him get away with that!"

"You're not looking at the big picture, Larry," Purdue said. "I'm not looking for revenge against this one man. If he leaves town, that's fine. If he works for the Simmonses, that's fine, too. Either way I'll know where he stands, and I'll know how to act."

"So we're just gonna wait and see."

"That's right, Larry," Purdue said, sitting behind his desk. "You'll learn patience this way. We're just going to sit and wait."

"What about Billy and Zack?"

"We'll keep them around for now," Purdue said, "along with the other two men. When it's all over, you'll fire all four of them. Understand?"

"No," Rhodes said, "I *don't* understand, but you're the boss."

"Just keep telling yourself that, Larry," Purdue said.

14

Before going to the laundry and getting into the alter-cation with Will Purdue's men, O'Grady had gone to the haberdasher's to order the clothes he would wear to the party. He had been told that it would take a few days, until he told the man that it was going on the Simmonses' bill.

"Is this for the party tonight?" the man asked.

"That's right."

"In that case," he said, "I'll have it ready by four."

O'Grady returned to the store at four and the man handed him his suit.

"Thanks very much," he told the man.

"See you at the party!"

O'Grady wondered if everyone in town was going to this party. He had heard several people talking about it during the day.

He also wondered if the Watson ranch was another place that Will Purdue was looking to take over.

He took the new suit of clothes back to his hotel and put them on. The man had taken very little time to measure him, yet the suit fit perfectly. This was obviously a man who knew what he was doing. The fit of the trousers was so good there would be no problem with his riding Cormac out to the ranch. Very often a good suit of clothes means riding in a buggy, or a buckboard.

At five o'clock he walked to the livery, had Cormac saddled for him, mounted up, and started for the Simmons ranch. Julia had given him directions that morning before she, Bo, and Mark had left town.

As he passed the sheriff's office, the man came out and stared at him.

"See you at the party," O'Grady said with a wave, even though he had no idea whether or not the man was invited.

The Simmons ranch was not as fancy as some of the big ranches O'Grady had seen around the country, but it was obviously a working ranch. The house was of the sort that a man would have built with his own two hands, rather than the kind of house a man like Will Purdue would *have* built for him.

O'Grady rode up to the front of the house and dismounted. Sitting on the porch was Mark Simmons, who waved with his good hand. O'Grady waved back and dismounted.

"I'll have somebody take care of your horse," Mark said. "We'll be going to the party by buggy."

O'Grady climbed the steps to the porch and saw that Mark was seated on a swing.

"Where's your sister?"

"Shh!" Mark said, holding his left index finger to his mouth and lowering his voice until Canyon could barely hear him. "She left already, to go and meet . . . Purdue."

O'Grady moved closer and said, "I guess she still hasn't talked to your father, huh?"

"Not about that—" Mark stopped short when the

front door opened. A big, barrel-chested man stepped out and stopped when he saw O'Grady.

"You must be the Canyon O'Grady I've heard so much about."

The man approached and extended a large, work-hardened hand. O'Grady shook it.

"Canyon, this is my father, Buck Simmons."

"We're all very grateful for what you did for Mark," Buck said. He released O'Grady's hand and placed his hand on Mark's shoulder. "Lord knows, though, I've wanted to break his arm once or twice myself."

They were all laughing when a beautiful, black-haired woman in her twenties came out of the house. She was wearing a colorful Mexican dress that fit her slender form very well, and yet was modest.

"Ah, my dear," Buck said. Now he removed his hand from Mark's shoulder and held his arm out to the woman. She moved close to him and he enveloped her.

With great pride on his face Buck Simmons said, "Mr. O'Grady, I would like you to meet my wife, Valeria. My dear, this is Canyon O'Grady, the man who broke Mark's arm."

"The man who saved his life, you mean," she said. She held her hand out to O'Grady, who took it and held it briefly. Her English was accented, but easily understandable.

"We are very grateful to you, Mr. O'Grady. I am also pleased that you will be attending the party with us. Another handsome man is always welcome. Now I will have three by my side."

"I am grateful for the invitation, Mrs. Simmons," O'Grady said, politely.

"Oh, please," she said, "after what you have done for this family you must call me Valeria."

"And you'll call me Buck," her husband said. "We don't stand on ceremony here. Of course, the person who invited you to the party is not here. I don't know what's got into that girl."

"It's all right, Buck," O'Grady said. "I certainly don't mind going with all of you."

"Well," Buck said, "we have time for a drink before we leave. My dear?"

"I would like a glass of sherry," Valeria said.

"Mr. O'Grady?"

"Sherry sounds fine."

Buck looked at his son and said, "A glass of lemonade for you, young man."

Mark didn't argue.

"I don't want anything to drink, anyway," he said to O'Grady and Valeria, when Buck went inside. "Not after last night."

"Good," Valeria said, "you've learned your lesson, then."

"Well," Mark said, giving O'Grady a wink, "for now."

Buck came back with a silver tray bearing three glasses of sherry and a glass of lemonade. He held out the tray so the others could take their drinks, then took the last one for himself.

O'Grady sipped it and nodded approvingly.

"It's excellent sherry."

"You sound like an educated man, Mr. O'Grady," Buck said. "Where are you from?"

O'Grady decided to simplify matters and not go too far into his background.

"I spend most of my time in Washington."

95

"Oh, I have always wanted to go to Washington," Valeria said, her eyes shining. "To see all the monuments, and the White House itself."

"You must let me know if you ever intend to come," O'Grady said. "I'll be glad to show you around."

They talked a little more about Washington, and when they had all finished their drinks Buck said, "I'll go and see about the buggy. The four of us will be able to fit quite well."

"Four?" O'Grady asked. "What about your brother, Bo?"

"My brother will make his own way," Buck said, and then added wryly, "he always has."

Buck went down the steps and crossed to the barn.

"Canyon, will you help me up out of this thing?" Mark asked.

O'Grady put his hand beneath Mark's left arm and lifted him out of the swing.

"Only reason they made me sit in that thing is because they knew I couldn't get up out of it by myself," the young man complained.

"Wouldn't you be better off staying behind?" O'Grady asked.

Mark grimaced in momentary pain and then said, "Probably, but when there's partying to be done I sure don't want to miss it."

"You'll have to sit, remember," Valeria said. "No dancing."

Mark looked at O'Grady and said, "She thinks she's my mother." He went down the steps without looking at his father's second wife.

O'Grady could see from the look on Valeria's face that the remark had hurt her.

"He didn't mean it," he said.

"Yes, he did," she said, shaking her head. There was a sad look on her face. "I can never convince him that I am not trying to replace his mother. Not with him, and not with my husband. I know my husband loved her dearly, and still does."

"What happened to her?"

"She became ill and died several years ago," Valeria said. "She helped my husband build all of this, but did not live to see it reach this level. For most of the years they were together it was small. It was only after she died that my husband began to become more successful."

"And now?"

She looked at O'Grady.

"He thinks I do not know that there are problems," she said. "He truly believes that he is shielding me from these things."

"And you let him go on believing it."

"Yes."

"And so you deceive each other."

She lifted her chin and looked at him boldly.

"I love my husband, Mr. O'Grady."

"Canyon," he said, "remember? And I don't doubt that you love each other, Valeria. I can see it in the way you look at him, and the way he looks at you."

Her expression softened and she said, "Thank you."

O'Grady saw Buck coming back, leading a horse and a four-seater buggy.

"It looks like it's time to go," he said to Valeria. He held his arm out to her and said, "Shall we?"

15

Although the Watson ranch was not as big as the Simmons place, the setup for the party certainly was impressive. There were rows of tables set up where people would eat, and a huge tent had been erected over them. Decorations hung from trees, the top of the tent, and the side of the house itself. There was music from strolling guitar and violin players, and the smell of barbecue hung heavy and pleasant in the air.

"Quite a turnout," O'Grady said, as he gazed at the many guests thronging the grounds.

"Oh, I think the whole town will be here," Buck said. He reined in the team, stepped down, and helped Valeria down. O'Grady descended and turned to give Mark a hand. A man came over and took the horse and the buggy off somewhere.

"I don't see Julia," Buck said.

O'Grady and Mark exchanged a glance. They both knew that Julia would probably walk in on Will Purdue's arm, but while Mark might have had some idea of how his father would react, O'Grady didn't.

Buck and Valeria went on into the tent to find their host, while O'Grady and Mark lay back.

"What's he going to do when he sees Julia with Purdue?" O'Grady asked Mark.

"You know, I'm not sure," Mark said. "He might go crazy, or he might take it real calm—and explode later."

"Let's hope he stays calm and doesn't make a scene here," O'Grady said.

"The food smells good," Mark said, "and there are already some pretty girls here. If you don't mind . . ."

"Go ahead," O'Grady said, "I was young myself, once . . ."

Left alone, O'Grady looked around and saw that Mark was right. There *were* a lot of pretty girls there. There were also some pretty *women*—and the one who was approaching him now was very familiar.

"Hello," she said.

He recognized her. It was Cora, the woman who owned the saloon. Tonight she was wearing a dress that, despite its rather modest design, showed off her full figure quite well. The men standing around were admiring it openly. She, however, was ignoring them.

"Hello, Cora," he said.

"Allen," she said. "It's Cora Allen."

"Canyon O'Grady."

"I remembered," she said. "I've been waiting for an interesting man to arrive."

"I'm flattered."

"No," she said, chuckling, "you're not. Let's have no false modesty, here."

"All right." He didn't mind playing the game when a woman wanted to, but it was always refreshing to find a woman who *didn't* want to.

"Would you like to help me find the punch bowl?" she asked.

"It would be my pleasure," he said.

She slid her arm in his and they walked off toward the tent.

"I saw you come in with the Simmonses," she said. "Is that a result of saving Mark's life last night?"

"Well," he said, "the result of saving Mark's life was being thrown in jail."

"So I heard."

"It was the Simmonses who got me out," he said. "So when Julia invited me to come here with them, I felt I had to accept."

"Julia, huh?" Cora said, with a raised eyebrow. "I didn't see her arrive with you."

"No," O'Grady said. "Uh, she's coming . . . later, I believe."

"I heard she was coming with Will Purdue," she said. "Is that true?"

"I'm sure I don't know."

She squeezed his arm and said, "I'm just as sure that you do. What do you think old man Simmons is going to do when he sees them?"

"Is everyone waiting around to see that?" he asked.

"Oh, yes," Cora said. "Most of the busybodies around here only came to see that. Afterward, half of them will probably leave."

"Good," O'Grady said as they reached the punch bowl. "More food, and punch, for us."

"Well," she said, accepting a glass of punch from him, "that's one way to look at it."

Julia Simmons was burning with anger. She sat in the buggy next to Will Purdue with her arms crossed beneath her breasts.

"Come on, Julia!" Purdue pleaded. "You're not

going to hold it against me that a little bit of business caused us to be late?"

"What kind of a fool do you take me for, Will Purdue?" she demanded.

"I don't know what you mean!" he protested, a look of innocence on his face.

"Of course you do!" she countered. "You made sure we would be late so that everyone would see us coming together—especially my father."

"Julia . . ."

"Don't try to deny it!"

"I'm *not* denying it!" he said. "But is that any different from you trying to get us to go early, so as *few* people as possible would see us?"

"Yes!"

"What's the difference?"

"I hate your guts," she said pointedly, "that's the difference."

"Come on, Julia," he said, putting his hand on her knee, "you don't mean that."

She slapped his hand hard. He laughed and removed it slowly.

"Keep your hand to yourself, Will, or you're going to lose it!"

"I'll remember that, Julia," he said. "I'll remember."

"What are you looking for?" Cora asked.

"I'm sorry," O'Grady said. He hadn't realized that he was looking beyond Cora.

"You make a gal try very hard, don't you, Canyon O'Grady?" she asked.

"Not usually," he said.

"Are you worried about Julia?"

"I'm worried about the whole situation, Cora," he answered.

"Oh, but not Julia specifically?"

"No."

"Good," she said. She put her hand on his arm and ran it up and down. "What would you say if I told you that when you and I leave here I'd like to go to your hotel room with you?"

He looked at her. Under normal circumstances, he wouldn't even have hesitated.

"Unfortunately," he said, "when I leave here I have to go back to the Simmons ranch to get my horse."

"That's all right," she said. "I'll wait for you in town. You see, I have no shame. When I see a man I want, I go after him, and I wanted you from the time I first saw you in my place."

He smiled at her and said, "You're a beautiful woman, Cora."

"But . . . ?"

He shook his head and said, "No 'buts.' All things being equal, I would love to have you come to my room when we get back to town."

"Well . . . good. That's what I was hoping to hear you say."

"Canyon . . ."

It was Mark Simmons. He had come up behind Canyon O'Grady with a glass of punch in one hand and a young girl on his other side. She smiled as O'Grady turned around.

"Look," Mark said, instead of making introductions.

O'Grady looked the way Mark was pointing and saw the buggy approaching.

"It's Purdue, with my sister," Mark said. "What do you want to bet he's coming late on purpose?"

"No bet," O'Grady said. "Where's your father?"

Mark looked around and said, "I'm not sure. He was talking to Mr. Watson for a while."

"Maybe he won't see them," O'Grady said.

"I doubt that," Mark said. "*Everyone* is going to see them."

"You got any friends around here?" O'Grady asked.

"Sure," Mark said, "lots of them. Lots of our men are here."

"Get them," O'Grady said.

"What?"

Putting his punch down, O'Grady said, "Get them. I've got an idea."

"What do I tell them?"

"Tell them to watch me," O'Grady said, "and do what I do."

"All right," Mark said. He handed the girl the glass of punch and said, "Excuse me, Wendy."

The girl looked confused.

"Excuse me, Cora."

"Sure," Cora said. "Go and do your good deed."

O'Grady hurried away, and Cora moved over next to the young and puzzled Wendy.

"Men!" Wendy muttered.

"Sweetie," Cora said, putting her arm around the girl's shoulder, "you don't know the half of it."

16

As the buggy approached, O'Grady started walking toward it. He looked behind him once to see how Mark was doing, and saw that men were already following him. Some of them looked confused, some curious, but they were all following his lead. By the time Will Purdue's buggy had reached the party, it was surrounded by a large group of men and almost hidden from sight.

"About *time* you made it, Julia," O'Grady said.

"Get away from here!" Will Purdue shouted.

"We'll give you a lift," O'Grady said to Julia.

He reached for her, and several other pairs of hands followed. They all lifted her from the buggy and carried her away. The other partygoers didn't know what was going on, they only knew that it sounded like someone was having a lot of fun. The laughing they heard was Julia's, as O'Grady and the other men from her father's ranch carried her away from Will Purdue, who was fuming and still shouting.

Purdue's men who were present at the party came running over, but by the time they'd reached their boss's side the others had dispersed. Purdue was standing up in his buggy, looking around either for Julia or for Buck Simmons.

Meanwhile, O'Grady and the others had carried Julia over to where her brother was standing and set her down next to him.

"Thanks, boys," she said to all of them. "I won't forget this."

"Well," O'Grady said, "he *did* escort you to the party."

"Was that your idea?" she asked her brother.

"I cannot tell a lie," Mark said. "It was Canyon's."

Julia looked at Canyon, and her smile was warm and dazzling.

"First you save my brother's life, and now mine. How can I thank you?"

"Before you thank me," O'Grady said, "let's be sure that we accomplished our purpose."

"To keep my father from seeing me arrive with Purdue," she said, looking around. "I don't see my father around, anywhere."

As Julia said that, the group saw Valeria Simmons approaching them with a bemused smile on her face.

"Come get some punch with me," Julia said to her brother, and they walked off before their stepmother could reach them.

"That was very clever of you, Canyon," she said.

"Where is your husband, Valeria?"

"He went inside with Mr. Watson some time ago, and has not yet returned. So you see, all of that was very unnecessary. He would not have been here to see them arrive together, anyway."

"Well, either way then," O'Grady said, "the plan worked."

"Why did she come with him, I wonder?" Valeria asked. "Do you know?"

"Yes I do, Valeria," he said. "It was the price Julia had to pay to get me out of jail."

He explained how she and Bo had wanted him out and Purdue had wanted him in, and since it was Purdue's men he had killed . . .

"I understand," she said. "Once again, Julia surprises me."

"How often does it happen?"

"Not very," she said, pulling a shawl close around her. "That is only because I usually expect the best from her, anyway. She is a very smart woman."

"Do the two of you get along?"

"Get along?" Valeria asked, thinking it over. "Yes, I think we 'get along' for the sake of her father. I do not think she likes me, but she does not shun me—usually."

"And Mark?"

"That is a somewhat different circumstance," she said, "as I described to you earlier."

"So Julia doesn't feel that you're trying to replace her mother?"

"No," Valeria said, "but neither does she like the fact that we are almost the same age—I *am* only a couple of years older than she is."

"I don't see where that makes a difference," O'Grady said, "if you and your husband are happy."

"Oh, I am very happy," she said, "and so is he, but he would also like the blessings of his children."

"Well," O'Grady said, "one day he may get them."

"I hope so," she said, "for his sake."

"And for your sake?"

She looked up at him and said, "I have my husband. I do not need their blessing to love him, or for him to love me. I am quite satisfied."

He watched her walk off and thought that she was a remarkable young woman. He also thought the same of Julia. He wondered, if Buck Simmons were not between them, if the two women could have become friends.

He turned and saw Will Purdue striding purposefully toward him. As annoyed as he had looked moments before, he now looked perfectly calm.

"Well orchestrated, Mr. O'Grady," he said. "Well done, indeed."

"I'm glad you appreciated it."

"Oh, I did," he said. "I appreciate cleverness in all its forms. I also appreciate a challenge, and that is what Julia presents to me, Mr. O'Grady. Were you to stay around for a while, you would also present a challenge to me."

"Unfortunately," O'Grady said, "I'm not."

"Really?" Purdue said. "Didn't Buck offer to pay you enough?"

"Buck hasn't offered me money," O'Grady said, "or a job."

"That's his error, then," Purdue said. "I won't make the same. Come and work for me. I'll pay you quite well."

"I'm sure you would, Mr. Purdue," O'Grady said. "I'm just not looking for a job."

"You have a job, then?"

"Do you mean, do I have a profession?"

"I suppose I mean that, yes," Purdue said. "Or perhaps I should just ask you how much longer you intend to stay around Eli's Crossing."

"Why?"

"Well, you do seem to be having some problems with my men."

"Oh, that reminds me," O'Grady said. He took out the gun he had taken off of Purdue's man earlier in the day. He had emptied it and tucked it into the back of his belt when he'd donned the suit.

"This belongs to one of your men, doesn't it?"

Purdue accepted it and said, "Yes, it does, and that shows you what I mean. If you stay here any longer I can't be responsible for what happens."

"Is that a threat?" O'Grady asked.

"I would never threaten you, Mr. O'Grady," Purdue said. "You strike me as the type of man to whom *that* would represent a challenge."

With that Purdue walked away, carrying the empty gun in his left hand. When he encountered his foreman coming the other way he thrust the gun toward him and waved at him to come and take it away.

"What was that all about?"

O'Grady turned to see Julia once again next to him. She was holding a glass of punch.

"He offered me a job."

"Why?"

"Because he thought I was working for your father," he said. "When I told him that I wasn't, he offered me a job."

"Did he offer you a lot of money?"

"He said he'd pay me a lot," O'Grady said. "We didn't get into particulars."

"Why not?"

"Because I'm not looking for a job."

"I see."

"Do they have anything stronger to drink than punch?" he asked.

She looked down at the glass in her hand, made a face, and said, "I certainly hope so."

"Let's go and find it."

Purdue turned and saw O'Grady walking away with Julia.

"Larry!"

Rhodes, who had been walking away, stopped and came back.

"Yeah, boss?"

"Has Bo Simmons gotten here yet?"

"No, boss."

"Good," Purdue said. He looked at Rhodes and said, "Get some of the men together."

"Why?"

"I want to give the Simmons family something to think about," Purdue said. Then he leaned into Rhodes and added, "Something to *worry* about."

"Something . . . fatal?" Rhodes asked.

Purdue eyed O'Grady and Julia again, and then said, "I guess that'll depend on how much of a fight he puts up."

"Bo Simmons?" Larry Rhodes said. "We're talking about something fatal."

"Get the men over here," Purdue said. "I'll talk to them myself."

"I'll go with them."

"No," Purdue said, "I want you and me to be seen here the whole time. You just pick the men and send them over to me. I'll handle the rest."

"Okay, boss," Rhodes said, "you got it."

17

O'Grady found the beer with Julia, and while they were waiting their turn at the keg he noticed Will Purdue talking to about five of his men. They were nodding while he spoke, and then they dispersed. As Canyon watched he was sure they were all taking different routes to the same place—their horses.

"I have to go," he said to Julia suddenly.

"What? Where?"

"Something's going on," he said, "and I want to find out what it is. Can you cover for me?"

"Cover for you? Why?"

"Because," he said, "I'm going to have to steal a horse."

"Steal—"

"Well, actually," he said, "borrow one. I'll bring it right back."

"Canyon, I—"

He left her standing there holding two steins full of beer.

He went in the general direction the other men had taken and found where all of the guests' horses had been picketed. In the distance he could hear horses rushing off, and it sounded like four or five.

He picked out a likely-looking animal and borrowed

it, untethering it and mounting up. There was a rifle in the scabbard, which might come in handy.

He didn't exactly know why he was doing this, except that he was following his instincts. What could Purdue have his men doing during the party, except something underhanded? He turned his borrowed horse in the direction the others had taken and kicked it into a full gallop.

Bo Simmons' mouth was dry. He was late for the party—*very* late—and it was all because of a mare who was in foal and had decided that *this* was the night to give birth. Once he'd gotten the foal out and cleaned off, he cleaned himself off, mounted up, and headed for the party.

It was dark, but there was enough moonlight for him to ride at a brisk clip. Abruptly, he heard horses heading toward him on the run, and he stopped to get a look. When he spotted them he saw four or five, headed straight for him. It took him even longer to realize that they were *not* his men, even though they were riding toward the ranch.

By the time he'd realized who they were, they were on him, and had taken him from his horse.

He knew he was in for a stomping. . . .

O'Grady had no difficulty following the sound of the running horses, and when he topped a rise and saw what was going on he knew who it was the five men were trying to beat into the ground.

He rode his horse hard into their midst. The animal knocked two down, and he leaped from his saddle and landed on a third.

The man they had been beating took advantage of

111

the opportunity to get to his feet, so that he could fight back better. In a split-second, O'Grady saw that he'd been right: Bo Simmons.

Over the next few minutes the two men fought against the five, actually holding their own by going back-to-back so no one could get behind them. O'Grady was dimly aware of his new clothes being torn to pieces, but that didn't seem to matter, considering that it might have been Bo Simmons getting torn to pieces, instead. It was a small price to pay, as were the cuts and bruises.

Finally, the five men grew tired. They weren't enjoying any great advantage—they had anticipated a five-against-*one* scrap—and finally one of them said "Fuck this!" and started running for his horse.

The others soon followed.

O'Grady and Bo Simmons sank to the ground, still back-to-back, breathing hard.

"We . . . should . . . go . . . after them," Bo Simmons said, wearily.

"I . . . know. . . ." O'Grady said, and neither man made a move to get up and give chase.

After a few moments they turned to face each other, but remained on the ground.

"How did you know?" Bo asked.

"I saw them talking with Purdue at the party," O'Grady said. "I knew something was up, but I didn't know what. Also, you weren't there yet. I just had a hunch."

"Well," Bo said, "I'm real glad you act on your hunches, Canyon. I give you my hand in thanks."

The two men shook hands weakly and then proceeded to climb to their feet, using each other for balance.

"I took somebody's horse," O'Grady said. "I hope it's got a canteen."

"I got somethin' better," Bo said.

They rounded up their horses, and then Bo reached into his saddlebag and came up with a flask.

"Whiskey," he said, handing it to O'Grady.

The agent accepted it and tipped it up, taking a couple of healthy swallows. The liquor burned through him and cleared his head.

He handed it back to Bo, who took three or four healthy swallows before he lowered the flask.

"You're making a habit of saving Simmons," Bo said, trying to catch his breath from the raw whiskey.

"Well, it's not something I set out to do," O'Grady said, "but I'm glad to be of help."

Bo frowned at him and said, "Is that your new suit?"

O'Grady looked down at himself and said, "Well, it *was*. I guess it doesn't look too good now, huh?"

"It looks terrible," Bo said, and then looked at himself and said, "And so do I."

"I can't go back to the party looking like this," O'Grady said.

"And I don't *feel* like goin' to a party anymore," Bo said. "What say you and me just head back home to the ranch?"

"Suits me," O'Grady said.

"I got some more whiskey there, too," Bo said, "and the cook can rustle us up somethin' to eat. By God, we'll have our *own* party."

Julia saw her father walking toward her, and she held her breath.

"You seen your uncle yet?" he asked.

"No, Pa," she said. "I don't think he's gotten here yet."

"I don't like it," Buck said. "Something's wrong."

"Maybe that mare decided to foal," Julia said.

"No," Buck said, "something's wrong."

"Well, I wouldn't agree with you, except . . ."

He looked at her quickly and said, "Except what?"

She told her father what Canyon O'Grady had done.

"When did he leave?"

"About half an hour ago."

"And *he's* not back yet?"

"No."

"All right," he said. "Find your brother, and I'll find Valeria. We're leaving."

"Yes, Pa."

He grabbed her arm as she started away and said, "And young lady, don't think I didn't see who you arrived here with. You've got a lot of explaining to do when we get home."

Her eyes widened, but she said simply "Yes, Pa" as he released her arm.

"Now go and get your brother," he said. "I'll make our excuses."

As she was running to find her brother she heard someone shout, "Hey, somebody stole my horse!"

18

When Buck Simmons pulled the buggy to a stop in front of the house, he stepped down and turned to help Valeria down behind him.

Mark climbed awkwardly to the ground, followed by Julia.

"Julia," Buck said, "take care of the horse and rig."

"I will, Pa," she said, "just as soon as we make sure that Uncle Bo is all right."

Buck stared at his strong-willed daughter and then said, "All right. Let's go inside."

They entered the house and Buck called out, "Bo! Bo, boy, where are you?"

"In here, John boy!" came Bo's ringing reply.

Buck frowned and followed the sound of the voice to the living room, followed closely by the others.

"Oh, my God!" Valeria exclaimed. "I'll get some water."

Buck waved at her, at a loss for words at the moment. His brother Bo and Canyon O'Grady were sitting on the sofa, looking for all the world like two men who had just gone through the wars. Their faces and arms were covered with cuts and welts and their clothes were in ruins, hardly more than rags hanging from their frames.

"Julia!" Valeria called.

Julia went and took the basin of water that Valeria was carrying and brought it into the living room.

"What in the name of God happened to you two?" Buck asked.

"Well," Bo said, "I was set upon by ten . . . fifteen yahoos and Canyon here—my good buddy, Canyon— came riding to my reshkew. Between us, we sent 'em off a-runnin'."

Buck looked at O'Grady and said, "He's drunk as a skunk. What's your story?"

"Well," O'Grady said carefully, "I don't think I'm drunk, although I *am* feeling kind of numb."

"It's a wonder you have any feeling at all," Valeria said, kneeling down in front of Bo. "Julia, take care of Mr. O'Grady."

Julia nodded and knelt in front of Canyon. With a wet cloth she started cleaning the cuts on his arms and face.

"Julia said you went running off from the party because you saw something," Buck said. "What did you see?"

"I saw Will Purdue send about five of his men away from the party on horseback," O'Grady said. "I had a feeling they were up to no good, so I borrowed a horse and followed them."

"Borrowed?" Buck said. "How about *stole*?"

"What's the difference?" Bo asked. "The point is he got to me before those, uh, twenty men could pound me into dogmeat."

"Five," O'Grady said, holding up five fingers. "There were five."

Bo lifted a whiskey bottle to his mouth, but Valeria snatched it away.

116

"That's enough of that," she said.

"Hey," Bo protested, "tha's my whiskey!"

"You want it?" she asked. She poured some on the cloth she was holding, then touched it to the biggest cut on his face.

"Ow!" Bo shouted, sitting straight up. "Lord, that hurt!"

"Sit still and stop being a baby," Valeria said.

Bo looked at her like he was seeing her for the first time and said meekly, "Yes, ma'am."

"Sit up," Julia said to O'Grady.

"Yes, ma'am," he said. He straightened up and placed both feet on the floor, so she could more easily reach his wounds. She was sitting between his knees.

"So you kept my fool brother from getting killed, huh?" Buck asked.

"Who you callin' a fool?" Bo demanded.

"Why were you so late for the party?" Buck demanded. "If you hadn't been riding around in the dark by yourself this wouldn't have happened."

"Tell it to that fool mare," Bo said. "She decided tonight was the time to have her baby."

"She had it?" Julia asked.

Bo smiled at her and said, "A bouncing baby colt, Julia."

"Yes," Julia said. "Canyon, are you hurt anywhere else?"

He stretched experimentally and said, "I don't think so."

"Stand up," she said.

He stood up, and suddenly a bolt of pain shot through his left foot.

"Christ!" he said, sitting down hard.

"Let me see," she said, lifting his leg. "That foot is swollen inside the boot."

"I didn't feel a thing until now," he said.

"You must have twisted it somehow." She turned and looked at her father. "We have to get that boot off."

"We'll have to cut it off," he said. "I'll get a knife."

O'Grady was trying to think back to the fight, and when he might have hurt his foot. All he could think of was the moment when he'd initially jumped off his horse. It *might* have happened then, and the pain just hadn't kicked in until now.

"This is great," he said, reaching down and rubbing his leg just above the boot. "I was going to leave tomorrow morning."

"Not on this foot you're not," Julia said.

"I have to be somewhere."

"It will have to wait."

Valeria finished with Bo and said, "There. At least you *look* better. Are you hurt anywhere else?"

"I got some sore ribs. . . ."

"Let me see," she said, reaching for his shirt.

"Ah, no, no," he said, pulling back from her, "I'll be fine, Valeria. Thank you for what you done."

"All right," she said, "suit yourself and be stubborn. I am going to make some coffee."

"Sounds good," O'Grady said.

Buck walked over to where his brother was sitting and said, "Sorry, Bo. I know the mare and her foal were important to you. I should have known you were late for a good reason."

Bo waved away his brother's apology and said, "Forget it, Buck."

"And you," Buck said, turning to O'Grady. "I

think you should have said something and got some help, but once again you've saved a member of my family."

O'Grady, too, waved Buck's words away.

"All right," Buck said, "let's get that boot cut off so your foot can breathe. . . ."

Julia, in preparing to rise from the floor in front of O'Grady, placed her hands on his thighs and pushed, and then realized what she was doing. She removed her hands as if touching him had burned her.

"Sorry," she said.

"No problem."

She carried the basin of water and the cloths from the room into the kitchen.

"Want to help with the coffee?" Valeria asked.

"I have to go out and take care of the horse and the rig," she said. "I promised Pa."

"Yes, that's right," Valeria said, "you did."

Julia stopped for a moment, as if she were going to say something to Valeria, then continued on and out the back door.

"You two look a little better," Buck said to O'Grady and Bo.

He had just finished cutting off O'Grady's boot and discarding it. He told O'Grady that he had a pair he could use.

The foot was swollen, but O'Grady was able to move his toes, so the injury didn't seem to be that serious.

O'Grady looked at Bo and said, "I think *he* looks a lot better."

Bo squinted at O'Grady and said, "So do you. I could use a drink, though."

"No more drinks," Buck said, seating himself next to Bo on the sofa. "I need you sober, so we can talk."

"About what?"

"About *what*? About Will Purdue sending his men after you!"

"What about it?"

"What's wrong with you, did they hit you in the head too many times?" Buck said.

"No, I got a hard head," Bo said. "I just don't see a problem here. Are you *surprised* that he sent his men after me?"

"Well . . . *yes*, aren't you?"

Bo looked at O'Grady, as if he wanted the agent to explain it to his brother—but that wasn't what he wanted, at all.

"Buck," he said, "you're so busy with your paperwork. I've been *expecting* Purdue to come after me—either me or Mark."

"Mark!"

"He wouldn't touch Julia," Bo said, "or Valeria. And you—well, you're the one he wants to crush *without* physically hurting you. To get to you he'd have to get to me or the boy."

"Last night he tried Mark," Buck said, through clenched teeth.

"I don't think so," O'Grady said. "I think it was a coincidence that Mark was there when Pete Webber came after me."

"But tonight," Bo said, "tonight was no coincidence. They came after me. They just wanted to give you something else to think about, Buck."

"Purdue apparently felt that with Bo laid up, or worse, you wouldn't be able to concentrate on keeping your ranch, or your land."

"Well, he's wrong," Buck said, with feeling. "That sonuvabitch—"

He stopped short when Valeria approached the room carrying a tray of coffee. She stopped at the door and looked at the three men.

"Am I interrupting anything?"

"No, my dear," Buck said. He stood up and walked over to take the tray from her.

She offered to leave, but Buck and Bo insisted that she stay and have some coffee with them.

O'Grady was wondering to himself just what it was that had made Purdue decide to go after Bo Simmons *tonight*. Was it because his plan of arriving with Julia at the party had been foiled by him? Was he, then, to blame for Bo's almost being seriously injured? And what of his own injuries, the worst of which seemed to be his foot? How long was that going to keep him off his feet? That remained to be seen in the morning.

"What are you thinking about, Canyon?" Valeria asked, handing him a cup of coffee. "You are frowning so."

"I'm thinking a lot of things, Valeria," O'Grady said.

"Personal things?"

"Some, yes."

She smiled and said, "Then I won't pry."

"Canyon's going to have to spend the night, Valeria," Buck said. "Would you get the guest room ready?"

"Yes, my husband."

She poured for her husband and her brother-in-law, and then for Julia, who had returned from taking care of the horse and rig. Mark had pleaded exhaustion and gone to bed already. After that, she went upstairs to prepare Canyon's bed.

"We'll have to get that horse I borrowed back to the owner, too," O'Grady said.

"I'll have that taken care of in the morning," Buck said. "Don't worry."

"I just don't want to end up in jail again," O'Grady said.

"You won't," Buck said. "That was Larry Johnson's horse. I'll talk to him."

"It's a good thing you picked a good horse," Bo said, "or you might not have gotten to me in time."

"I hope you won't be missing anything in town tonight," Julia said to him.

He looked at her to see if there was any hidden meaning there. Did she know about him and Cora? Maybe she had seen them talking together and just assumed that they were . . . involved.

"No," he said, "I'm not missing anything in particular."

"Well," Julia said, looking him straight in the eye, "good."

19

Will Purdue looked down at the woman lying next to him. He hadn't expected to bring a woman home with him from the party last night, but it had happened, and he wasn't sorry. True, Cora Allen wasn't Julia Simmons, but she certainly was good in bed.

Cora had been angry because Canyon O'Grady had been seen riding away. She assumed that he would not be meeting her in town, and she had started drinking.

Purdue had also been drinking, because Julia Simmons was pointedly ignoring him, and because he was angry with Canyon O'Grady for having ruined his entrance. Also, Rhodes had seen O'Grady riding out right after Purdue's men. This morning Purdue would find out if his men had done their job on Bo Simmons.

Cora moaned, and Will lowered the sheet so that he could see her smooth butt. He ran his hand over it, letting his middle finger trail along the crease between her buttocks, and then down lower and around until he had his finger in a wet and warm spot.

"Oooh," Cora moaned, waking and rubbing her belly into the mattress as he probed her with his finger. "Oooh, God," she said, and rolled over.

She reached for Purdue and took hold of him, rubbing gently at first, then more insistently.

He growled, pushed her hand away, and mounted her. He poked into her easily, piercing her fully, and began to move in her, slowly at first, and then harder and harder until he was literally pounding away at her.

She cried out, wrapping her legs around his waist while he slid his hands beneath her to cup her buttocks.

As he took her he closed his eyes and pretended that she was Julia Simmons. . . .

"Come downstairs when you're ready," Purdue told Cora as he dressed. "I'll have the cook make you some breakfast."

"For both of us?" Cora asked from the bed.

Purdue didn't look at her.

"I have some work to do," he said. "I'll probably have breakfast later."

"That's okay," she said. "I have to get back to town. I have a business to run."

He looked at her then and said, "Yes, I suppose we both do."

She nodded, held his glance for a moment, and then watched as he walked out, closing the door gently behind him.

She rolled over in bed and looked around the room. It was the first time she'd realized that this could not be his bedroom. A man like Purdue would have a much larger and fancier decorated room. He had chosen to take her here—probably a guest room—rather than to his own bed.

Well, she thought, rubbing her hands over her face, *I guess that puts me in my place.*

* * *

Purdue went downstairs and outside, looking for Larry Rhodes.

"Palmer!" he called out to a man who was passing the house.

"Yes, sir?"

"Tell Rhodes I want him. Now!"

"Yessir!"

Purdue went back inside and told the cook he'd be in his office and wanted a cup of coffee. She brought it to him, and he was about to take his first sip when Rhodes showed up at his door. Purdue put his cup down and stared at the man, knowing instinctively that something had gone wrong.

"What?" he said.

"O'Grady."

"What?"

"He got there before they could finish their job," Rhodes said with a shrug.

"That's why he went riding out last night," Purdue said. "How did he know?"

Rhodes didn't have an answer.

Purdue looked at his foreman angrily and asked, "What do I pay these men for? There were still *five* of them against two!"

"Boss," Rhodes said, "we know how tough Bo Simmons is. Apparently, O'Grady is in the same class."

"Yeah, well," Purdue said, "maybe if *I* had a few men like that things would be different. Jesus! I ask for a simple thing to be done. . . ."

Rhodes didn't reply. He knew—and he knew that Purdue knew—that giving a beating to Bo Simmons was no simple thing.

"They're lucky they all came back alive," Rhodes said to Purdue.

Purdue pinned him with a hard stare and said, "Maybe they won't think they're so lucky when I get through with them."

"Boss . . ."

"All right, all right, just get out," Purdue said, waving the man away.

On his way to the front door, Rhodes saw Cora coming down the stairs. He was not surprised. He had seen her ride back with Purdue in the buggy.

"Good morning, Cora."

"Larry," she said, with a smile. "Do you think you could get someone to take me back to town?"

"Sure, Cora," Rhodes said. "No problem."

Out on the front porch he asked, "You and the boss, uh, got something . . ."

"No, no," she said, smiling. "I think last night we were both just wishing the other one was someone else—if that makes any sense."

"I guess it does," Rhodes said, thinking of Julie Simmons. Somehow, he thought that if *he* were Purdue he could make do with Cora Allen.

"And then again," she said, shaking her head sadly, "maybe it doesn't."

Will Purdue sat back in his chair and stared at the wall in front of him.

He was beginning to grow very impatient. Impatient waiting for the bank to foreclose on Buck Simmons; impatient waiting for Julia Simmons to come around to his way of thinking; and *now,* impatient with Canyon O'Grady. Three times O'Grady had had altercations with his men and had come out on top. He either had to send in more men—although Lord knows, you'd think that *five* was enough—or else hire better men. More expensive men.

Specialists.

Yeah, he thought, *but the kind of specialists you have in mind do only one thing for money—kill.*

Up to now there had been no killing, but Will Purdue was getting tired of waiting, tired of trying to do things the right way.

Maybe the time had finally come to just *take* what he wanted.

20

When O'Grady woke the next morning, his first thought was of his foot. If he stood up and it held, then he might still be able to leave and get to Hastings before his deadline. If he couldn't leave, then he was going to have to send a telegraph message to Rufus Wheeler in Washington and explain why. He didn't relish the thought of having to do that.

Gingerly, he tried moving his toes, and they worked. The next step was to toss back the covers and take a look at the foot. He did so, and although it still looked swollen it didn't look as bad as he'd thought it might.

The final step was to simply stand up and try it. He brought both feet around to the floor, which was cold against his bare soles. He took a deep breath, stood up, and let his weight rest on both feet.

The pain was not sharp, but it was still there. He knew his own body well enough to know that trying to put a boot on that foot, and then walking on it, was not going to be easy.

He also knew that he was going to try it, anyway.

O'Grady managed to make his way downstairs, fully dressed but barefoot. He wanted to find Buck Simmons, because the man had said he would give him a pair of boots.

In moving around and getting dressed, O'Grady had discovered other aches and pains aside from the pain in his foot. When he looked down at himself, he saw that his torso was covered with welts and bruises. Somehow he had managed to get a huge purplish bruise on his left thigh. Since that was also the ankle that was injured, he had to assume it had happened at the same time—again, most likely when he had jumped from the saddle into the fight.

There didn't seem to be anyone around. He figured, since this was a working ranch, that meant that everyone was already out and about, and not that they were sleeping late. He walked to the front door, opened it, and stepped outside.

He saw the hands moving about, tending to their daily chores. There was a cool breeze in the air, and he liked the way it felt on his face and on his bare feet. He moved over to the swing/bench and sat down on it. He figured he'd just wait for one of the family members to come along. It was just about six A.M. Breakfast would be served soon.

He was surprised when the first person he saw was Mark Simmons, but then Mark came from inside the house. That meant that he had probably gotten out of bed even after O'Grady.

"Morning," Mark said, sitting down next to O'Grady on the swing.

"How's the arm?" O'Grady asked.

"Hurts like hell," Mark admitted. "Looks like you didn't fare too well last night."

"I'm okay," O'Grady said. "Some bumps and bruises, and a sprained ankle."

"Gonna be able to leave today?"

"I don't think so," O'Grady said. "Your father said he had a pair of boots for me."

"Pa's got a big foot," Mark said. "If you sprained your ankle, you'll need a bigger boot, anyway."

"Right."

Suddenly O'Grady saw Julie Simmons coming toward them, apparently from the barn.

"Here comes Julie," Mark said. "Must be gettin' close to breakfast. Her stomach can usually tell."

Julie came up the steps, stopped, and looked at the two injured men sitting on the swing.

"How sweet," she said. "Except I suspect I'd usually find one of you sitting with a girl, and not together."

"There's room," O'Grady said, moving to his right to make a small amount of room between him and Mark.

"No thanks," she said. "Three on a swing is a crowd. I'm going inside to check on breakfast."

"Where is everybody?" Mark asked.

"I don't know," Julie said, "but I'd bet money that Pa and Bo will be here soon."

"Sure," Mark said. "They've got stomachs like yours."

"Ha!" Julie said. "You're the only one who *doesn't* seem to have the Simmons stomach, Mark."

Mark smiled and patted his flat stomach with his good hand.

"That's why I'll always be thin and beautiful, sister dear."

"Ouch!" she said, clutching her stomach. "That's hitting below the belt . . . *brother* dear!"

With that Julie went inside, and O'Grady and Mark shared a laugh.

"She likes you," Mark said.

"What?"

"Julie," Mark said, "you know, my sister? She likes you a lot."

"How can you tell?" O'Grady asked.

"Oh, the way she looks at you," he said, "the way she talks when she's around you. Why, can't you tell?"

"Well . . ."

"You like her, too, don't you?"

"Well, sure I do, Mark," O'Grady said. "So far I like everybody in your family."

"Oh yeah," Mark said, nodding, "and you like us all the same, right? You don't like *Julie* just a little more than the rest of us?"

"Well," O'Grady said, "let's just say that I don't have the same *feelings* when I'm looking at the rest of you that I have when I look at your sister."

"Well, good," Mark said. "Why don't you stand up and give me a hand out of this swing, and *we'll* go and check on breakfast, too."

"Sounds good to me," O'Grady said.

As they entered the house Mark said, "I heard Pa talking to Valeria about you last night."

"When?"

"At the party."

"What was he saying?"

"That Julia could do worse than you," Mark said. "He saw her arrive with Purdue, you know, even after what you pulled."

"I didn't know that."

"Yeah," Mark said, "he said he was looking out the window of the house and saw them ride up, before the mob scene."

"What did he say to Julia?"

"He told her he knew, but I don't think they've, uh, discussed it, yet. I think what happened with you and Buck last night kept them from it."

"I hope he's not too hard on her," O'Grady said. "I'd feel responsible. After all, she did it for me."

"Yeah," Mark said, giving O'Grady an elbow, "and that was before she decided she liked you so much."

As predicted, both Buck and Bo showed up just as breakfast was being served.

"How's your foot, Canyon?" Buck asked as he entered the dining room.

"Still sore, but not as swollen."

"Well, I'll get you that pair of boots right after breakfast."

"I'd appreciate it, Buck," O'Grady said. He looked at Bo, whose face looked somewhat worse than his did, due to the blows he had taken before O'Grady arrived. "How are you feeling, Bo?"

"Sore as hell," Bo said, sitting down at the table, "but that don't ever keep me from working." He reached for the bowl of scrambled eggs in the center of the table and winced at the pain it caused his ribs. Apparently, the worst of his injuries couldn't be seen.

Valeria was the last to arrive for breakfast.

"I am sorry I am late, everyone," she said.

"No one's complaining, Valeria," her husband assured her. He looked around the table to make sure that he was correct.

They passed around bowls of eggs and grits and potatoes, platters of bacon and ham, and baskets of biscuits. It was arguably the best breakfast O'Grady had had in months—maybe years.

He noticed Buck and Julia exchanging glances during the meal. It appeared to him that Buck wanted to talk about last night, but maybe not in front of everybody.

Finally, Buck spoke. "Julia, after breakfast I'd like to talk to you in my office. All right?"

She looked across the table at him and said, "Sure, Papa," then bit her lip.

"Canyon," Bo said, "how would you like to go into town with me?"

"As long as I can walk, that sounds like a good idea," O'Grady said. "I think I'm going to have to send a telegraph message, anyway."

"And we'll pick up your gear from the hotel," Bo said. "You might as well stay out here until you're ready to move on."

O'Grady considered saying no, but then figured, why not? Besides, there was safety in numbers. Maybe out here he wouldn't run into any more of Will Purdue's men.

21

When Buck and Julia Simmons went into Buck's office, Bo said to O'Grady, "This is a good time to leave, boy. I'll get those boots Buck promised you."

Bo came down with the boots, which were too big for O'Grady, so his swollen foot fit right in. It was the other boot that was loose, but not loose enough to be a problem—as long as he didn't have to run.

"How's it feel?"

"Good," O'Grady said, meaning his injured foot. "Let's see how it feels as the day passes."

They went out to the barn and saddled their horses. O'Grady noticed that the horse he had "borrowed" the night before was gone, and he mentioned it.

"Yeah," Bo said, saddling his own roan, "we had it taken back first thing this morning. I don't think you'll be arrested."

"Well, that's a relief."

When they mounted up, O'Grady used his arms more than usual to take the pressure off his left foot, which went into the stirrup first. It was still pretty painful, though.

"What do you think Buck is saying to Julia?" O'Grady asked.

Bo looked over at O'Grady and said, "I *never* know

what my brother's gonna say, Canyon. That's just the way he is."

Julia was surprised. She had thought that her father would start shouting as soon as he'd closed the door. Instead he walked around his desk, sat down, and pressed his clasped hands to his mouth.

"Pa?"

"Julia," he said, shaking his head, "I'm sure you had a good reason to do what you did. In fact, Bo told me what the reason was. You wanted to get O'Grady out of jail because he saved Mark's life."

"That's right."

"That's admirable."

She stared at her father and said, "It is? You mean . . . you're not mad?"

"Oh yes," he said, "I *am* mad. In fact, I'm *damned* angry."

"But you just said . . ."

"I said it was an admirable thing to do, and it was," he said, "but you didn't tell *me* what you did. *That's* what I'm angry about!"

She looked down at her feet sheepishly and said, "I know, Pa—"

"Don't you *dare* call me Papa!" he said, cutting her off.

She lifted her head and stared at him in surprise. *Now* that famous Buck Simmons temper was threatening to come out.

"Why did you think you couldn't tell me?" he demanded.

"I don't know . . . Pa," she said. "I guess I thought you might think I had done something wrong."

"Right or wrong," he said, "you gave your word.

There wasn't much I could do about it. You *did* only offer to go to the party with him, right?"

"Of *course*," she said. "What else do you think I would do?"

"I don't know."

"Pa," she said, "you *know* me better than to think I'd do anything like . . . like *that*."

Now it was Buck's turn to look sheepish.

"I know, honey."

"Pa," she said, "nothing happened, and nothing is going to happen—not between me and Will Purdue."

"All right," he said. He stood up, came around the desk, and held out his arms. "All right," he said again as he held her, "but if nothing is going to happen between you and Purdue, how about you and Canyon O'Grady?"

She pushed back from him, looked at him in surprise, and exclaimed, "Daddy!"

"Now, honey . . ."

"Are you trying to match me up with Canyon?"

"I have eyes, Julia," Buck said. "So do Valeria, Bo, and Mark. We have all seen the way the two of you look at each other."

"I can't believe this. . . ." Julia said, shaking her head.

"Look," Buck said, "all I'm saying is that you could do worse for yourself. He's obviously a good man, or else why would he risk himself for us all these times?"

"I don't know," she said. "Maybe one of us should ask him."

"What?"

"Maybe there *is* something he wants, and it's just that none of us have asked him."

Buck frowned.

"All right, then," he said after a moment, "*you* ask him."

"Why me?"

"Because you thought of it," he said. "Because *you're* the suspicious one, girl."

"Well, *somebody* in this family has to be suspicious," she said.

"Then it's settled," he said. "You have a talk with O'Grady . . . about a lot of things."

"All right," she said. "About a lot of things *of my choosing*."

Buck spread his arms out and said, "It's in your hands, Julia. I trust you."

Julia shook her head in wonderment at her father and left his office.

In the front entryway she ran into her brother.

"Did he tear off your hide?" Mark asked.

"No," Julia said, in a tone that betrayed her puzzlement, "he was very understanding—and a little hurt that I had tried to keep it from him."

"But not angry?" Mark asked, in surprise.

"Well, not *too* angry."

"It wasn't so bad, then."

"I wouldn't say that, either."

"What do you mean?"

She put her hands on her hips and asked, "What have you been telling him about Canyon O'Grady?"

"I like Canyon," Mark said. "I think he's a good, steadying influence on me, don't you think?"

"You know what I mean, Mark," she said, scolding him. "What have you been telling Pa about O'Grady and *me*?"

"Oh. Jeez, you know, my arm really hurts," he said, edging towards the stairs.

"Oh, no!" she said, grabbing his good arm. "You better talk, or I'll break *this* one!"

"Okay, okay, let go!" he said, reclaiming the arm while it was still healthy.

"Talk."

"I haven't said anything," he said. "Pa asked me what I thought about you and Canyon."

"And?"

"I said that the two of you couldn't seem to stop looking at each other."

"That's silly."

"And he agreed."

"Then you're both mad," she said. "It's not that way at all."

"Okay, it's not," he said. "Can I go now?"

"Go," she said. "Run!" As he went up the stairs, she said "coward" under her breath, but then smiled and started to shake her head.

It was no secret that her father wanted her to get married. There just weren't any good prospects around. At one time she had *thought* Will Purdue was a prospect, but she'd quickly changed her mind about that. Since then she hadn't even been *attracted* to a man. Until now. Okay, so she *was* attracted to Canyon O'Grady, but he certainly didn't seem to be the marrying kind. Since his arrival, he'd been looking forward to leaving.

Of course, it *would* be a shame not to at least get to know him a little better before he left. . . .

22

On the ride to town, Bo broached the subject of Julia to O'Grady.

"What do you think of Julia, Canyon?" he asked. His attempt at framing an "innocent" question was so pitiable as to be laughable.

"You, too?"

Bo looked at O'Grady and said, "What do you mean, 'me too'?"

"Mark was playing matchmaker this morning," O'Grady said.

"Matchmaker?" Bo said, frowning. "I ain't playin' matchmaker. I'm just askin' you a simple question. Jesus, a body would think I was askin' you to *marry* my niece."

"Bo," O'Grady said, "I'm very impressed with Julia."

"Does that mean you like 'er?"

"Yes," O'Grady said, "that means I like her."

"Well then . . ."

"Can we talk about something else?"

Bo, looking insulted, said, "Hmph! A body tries to make a little conversation, and he gets his head bit off for his trouble."

"I'll make conversation," O'Grady said. "What's the real reason we're going to town this morning?"

"Oh, that," Bo said. "Well, I'd sort of like to run into Will Purdue today, or somebody from his ranch, but the real reason is to talk to the sheriff."

"About last night?"

Bo nodded.

"Buck thinks it's a good idea," Bo said. "Personally I think it's a waste of time, because the goddamned *sheriff* of this town is a waste of time, but Buck says it'll look better for us if trouble starts—I mean *real* trouble."

"Does Buck think it will come to that?" O'Grady asked.

"I been waitin' for it to come to that for a long time, Canyon," Bo said. "Purdue's had these two-bit gunmen on his payroll for a long while, the ones you tangled with, and the ones *we* tangled with."

"Well, so far I haven't been real impressed with the caliber of his men."

"Well, no matter how good or bad they are," Bo said, "if he sends enough of them the job will get done. If he had sent ten men last night instead of five, you and me wouldn't be here right now."

"That's true enough."

"Sometimes," Bo said, "I figure maybe it would be best if I just went and killed Purdue myself."

"You'd be on the run then, Bo."

Bo looked at O'Grady and said, "I been on the run before."

By the time they had reached town O'Grady was starting to have second thoughts. His aches and pains were not so bad, and the foot had stood up to the hour-long ride fairly well. He could still leave town today and possibly make it to Hastings in time for his deadline.

They rode up to the livery stable and left their horses there to be cared for. Since Bo was going to see the sheriff, and O'Grady was going to send a telegram and pick up his gear, they figured they might as well put the horses up for most of the day.

"We can stop in the saloon, too, while we're here," Bo said, rubbing a hand over what seemed to be his eternally dry lips as they walked away from the livery.

"It's a little early for that, Bo."

"It is?" Bo asked. "Well, we *could* wait until noon . . . I guess."

"Why don't you go and talk to the sheriff?"

"Maybe we both should," Bo said. "Remember, we was *both* there last night."

"All right," O'Grady said. "I'll go to the telegraph office afterward."

Bo nodded, and they headed for the sheriff's office.

Sheriff Zeke Harrison looked up from his desk as the door to his office opened, then looked away when he saw Bo Simmons and Canyon O'Grady enter. *What,* he asked himself, *have I done to deserve this*? The answer was obvious. He had accepted the job of sheriff.

"What can I do for you gents?"

"You can throw Will Purdue in jail, for one thing," Bo Simmons started.

"Mr. Purdue?" Harrison asked.

"Look at him," Bo said to O'Grady. "Just mention the man's name and his knees start shaking." He leaned on Harrison's desk and shouted, "You're supposed to be the sheriff, man! Act like one!"

"W-what are you talking about?"

"Last night Will Purdue sent five men out to kill me," Bo said. "If it wasn't for Canyon O'Grady here, they would have, too."

"How do you know they were Mr. Purdue's men?" Harrison asked.

"Who else *would* they be?" Bo shouted, but O'Grady knew that was the wrong answer.

Harrison, sensing this, looked at O'Grady.

"Did you recognize any of the men?"

"I haven't been in town long enough to know all of his men," O'Grady said. "It was dark."

Bo gave O'Grady an exasperated look and said, "Do you *have* to tell the truth?"

"Bo," Harrison said, trying to at least *sound* like a sheriff, "I can't do a thing unless you can identify these men as working for Mr. Purdue—and even then I'd only be able to take action against *them*, not him."

"They *work* for him."

"When your men come to town and bust up the saloon, do I throw *you* in jail?"

Bo opened his mouth to reply, then realized that there *was* no reply. He looked to O'Grady for help, but the big redheaded agent could only shrug.

"You're the one who told him to act like a sheriff," he reminded Bo.

"Bo," Harrison said, "if you see one of the men who attacked you, you let me know and I'll question him."

"Can't you question Purdue?"

The thought of questioning Purdue obviously caused the sheriff some problem.

"Oh, uh, well, if it turns out that his men *did* attack you—and you can identify them—uh, I guess I'll *have* to question him. . . . But that don't mean I have to bring him in here."

"No," Bo agreed, "it don't."

"Come on, Bo," O'Grady said, "we've done all we can do here."

Reluctantly, Bo followed O'Grady out.

"Can you believe that little weasel?" he demanded when they were outside.

"He's doing his job, Bo."

"Yeah," Bo said, "for *once*! But does he have to pick *now* to act like a real sheriff? He threw you in jail quick enough!"

"That was different," O'Grady said. "There were a lot of witnesses who saw what happened."

"So?" Bo said. "There were two of us last night who saw what happened."

"Can you honestly remember the face of one of those men from last night?"

Bo thought hard and then admitted grudgingly, "No."

"Then there's not much we can do."

Bo frowned.

"Look," O'Grady said, "I've got to go and send a telegraph message. I'll meet you at my hotel."

"Hell, I'll come with you," Bo said. "The saloon ain't open yet, and I got nothin' else to do."

"Well," O'Grady said, "if you want to," although he didn't really want the other man to go with him. It was going to be hard enough explaining to Wheeler in Washington why he was going to be late to Hastings. Wording the telegram would be even harder with Bo Simmons looking over his shoulder.

"Wait a minute," Bo said.

"What?"

"I can go over to the general store," he said. "We got to order some supplies for the ranch, anyway."

"Oh . . . okay."

"So I'll meet you at your hotel, after all."

"Fine," O'Grady said. "See you there in about half an hour."

O'Grady finally decided to mention the names of all of the people he had become involved with in his telegram to Wheeler. Even without Bo looking over his shoulder he had to be careful, because he didn't want the operator spreading it around town that he had sent a telegram to a Major General whose office was in the White House.

Wheeler maintained a separate address for such telegraph messages. O'Grady gave the operator that address, then dictated his message.

"Tied up in Eli's Crossing with Buck Simmons and Will Purdue dispute. Sustained slight injury, will be late for next appointment. Please advise."

"That's it?" the operator asked.

O'Grady thought a moment, then said, "Yes, that'll do it."

The operator tallied up what O'Grady owed, then asked where O'Grady would be when the reply came.

"Try the hotel first," O'Grady said, "and if I'm not there, the saloon."

"Expectin' the answer soon?"

Knowing Wheeler, O'Grady said, "Probably *real* soon."

"Okay, mister," the man said. "I'll find you when it comes in."

"Thanks."

O'Grady left, wondering whether or not Wheeler's reply would literally burn up the telegraph wires.

The telegraph key operator, whose name was Shep Stone, watched carefully as Canyon O'Grady left the office and walked off down the street. He even walked to the door to look out and make sure that the man wasn't coming back.

After that he sat down, keyed the message in and made sure it was received, then locked the key and left the office. In his hand he held a copy of Canyon O'Grady's message.

23

When Buck Simmons came out of his office that morning, he walked around the house looking for Julia, or Mark, or Bo, or even Canyon O'Grady. Nobody was around, and he was starting to think that everyone had deserted him.

He went outside and started looking around. He finally found Julia *and* Mark down at the barn, looking over the new foal.

"Where's your Uncle Bo?" he asked.

Julia was sitting on the ground with the foal. Mark, cradling his arm, was standing and watching. He turned at the sound of his father's voice.

"Uncle Bo rode into town, Pa," Mark said, "while you were talking to Julia."

"What?" Buck said. "He went to town alone? After what happened last night? And what about O'Grady?"

"He went with him," Mark said.

"Those two idiots!" Buck said. "They're setting themselves up as targets again!"

Julia stood up and said, "Uncle Bo wouldn't do that on purpose, would he, Pa?"

Buck stared at Julia and said, "You know your Uncle Bo, Julia. You tell me."

"I'll saddle the horses," she said.

*　*　*

When O'Grady got to the hotel, Bo Simmons wasn't there yet. He walked up to the front desk.

"Would you prepare my bill?" he asked the clerk. "I'll be checking out."

"Yes, sir," the man said. "I hope you enjoyed your stay."

"It's been interesting."

He went up to his room and started collecting his gear. When he returned to the lobby, Bo was there waiting.

"Get our supplies ordered?"

"All taken care of," Bo said. He rubbed his hand over his mouth and said, "Why don't we check and see if the saloon is open?"

"I'll take my gear over to the livery and leave it with my horse," O'Grady said.

"Okay," Bo said, "I'll help you."

"I think you forgot about something, Bo."

"What's that?"

"Vince Gill."

"Holy sh—you're right. I *did* forget about Vince. We'll have to take him back to the ranch with us."

"Why don't you go up and see him while I take my gear over to the livery?"

"Why don't we *both* go up and see him?" Bo said. "I think Vince likes you."

"You think so?"

"Yeah," Bo said, then added, "course, not as much as Julia. . . ."

"Let me pay my bill."

Bo took O'Grady's rifle and saddlebags while the big redhead paid his bill.

When O'Grady turned and reached for his things, Bo said, "I got it! How's your foot?"

"Now that you mention it," O'Grady said, "it's pretty sore."

"Think you could make the ride to Hastings?"

They started up the stairs, with O'Grady favoring the injured ankle.

"Well, I wouldn't be walking, I'd be riding," O'Grady said, "but I've already sent my telegram explaining that I'll be a little late. I think I can wait one day and leave tomorrow."

Upstairs, they walked to Gill's room and knocked on the door.

"It's open."

They walked in and found Gill sitting up in bed.

"You been leaving the door unlocked like that all night?" Bo asked.

"Nah," Gill said. "The doc was here earlier and he left it unlocked. Are we ready to go back to the ranch?"

"Probably a little later on," O'Grady said. "We just wanted to let you know we didn't forget you."

Bo gave O'Grady a look.

"You two look like you been through the mill," Gill said. "What happened?"

Bo looked at O'Grady, who motioned for him to tell the story.

"Sounds like you had a high old time," Gill said. "Sorry I missed it—and I'm sorry I missed the party."

"There'll be other parties," Bo said. "Look, we'll be back for you later in the afternoon, okay?"

"I'll be ready."

They went back downstairs and left the hotel.

"You're walkin' funny," Bo said.

"Well, my ankle hurts, and the other boot is too big and keeps slipping."

"Might want to buy another pair before leaving town," Bo suggested.

"You might be right."

They went to the livery, dropped O'Grady's gear off next to his saddle, and then walked over to the saloon, which—to Bo's great satisfaction—was open.

"Beer?" Bo asked.

"Fine."

"I'll get it," he said. "Sit at a table."

Not only did O'Grady sit at a table, but he pulled off Buck Simmons' boots. As he was waiting for Bo to get the beers, a door in the back opened and Cora Allen stepped out. It was then that he remembered that he'd been supposed to get together with her last night after the party.

She spotted him and walked over. She was wearing a simple shirt and skirt, with boots. Nothing provocative, but she was a provocative-looking woman no matter what she wore. He stood up when she had reached the table.

"Well," she said, putting her hands on her hips, "I'm glad to see you alive"—she eyed his bootless feet—"and comfortable. Where did you run off to last night?"

"I'm sorry, Cora," he said, "but something came up. I, uh, managed to hurt my ankle. . . ."

"And your face, from the looks of it," she said. She put her hand beneath his chin and lifted, giving his face the once-over. "You better sit down and take your weight off that ankle."

He did so and said, "I appreciate you not being angry."

"About being stood up?" she asked, with a smile. "I made other arrangements when I saw you go riding off. Besides, you *do* have a good reason, don't you?"

"Hello, Cora," Bo said as he joined them. He set the two beers down on the table and remained standing. "He sure *does* have a good reason. He saved my bacon last night."

"Hello, Bo. Did he, really?"

"Five of Will Purdue's boys tried to put an end to my misery, but O'Grady got there in time. Together, we made *them* miserable."

"I see," Cora said. "This Purdue/Simmons thing is really escalating into a feud, isn't it?"

"No feud," Bo said, sitting down. "Purdue is just starting to push too hard. Sooner or later you gotta push back, you know?"

"It makes sense to me," she said. She looked at O'Grady and said, "Are you leaving town today, as you planned?"

He decided not to try to explain why he was leaving the hotel and moving out to the Simmons ranch.

"Yes," he said, "I am leaving town," which was not a lie.

She nodded and said, "Well, you boys enjoy your beers, hear?"

"That's quite a woman," Bo said, watching her walk away.

"Do I detect some interest there, Bo?"

Bo turned his head and stared at O'Grady in surprise.

"Me? Why would I think that a woman like that would be interested in a wreck like me?"

"I don't know," O'Grady said, with a shrug. "You never know unless you ask, do you?"

Bo frowned and sipped his beer, then rubbed his jaw thoughtfully.

"Message from Shep, the guy at the telegraph office," Rhodes said as he entered Purdue's office. "It pays to keep him on the payroll."

Purdue accepted and read the copy of Canyon O'Grady's message.

"Doesn't look like O'Grady's plannin' to leave, does it?" Rhodes asked.

Purdue put the message down on his desk and said, "No, it doesn't, does it?"

"He's in town right now."

Purdue nodded.

"With Bo Simmons."

Purdue looked interested.

"Want me to send some boys into town?"

Purdue thought it over. He certainly didn't have to send for some real talent. He and Rhodes had already talked about using *enough* men for the job the next time.

"All right," he said. "Send ten this time."

"And?"

"And," Purdue said, looking at Rhodes, "take *care* of it, Larry."

"I'll go along, too," Rhodes said, "to . . . supervise."

"Whatever," Purdue said, with a wave of his hand. "This time I'm leaving it in your hands."

"Right, boss."

As Rhodes started for the door Purdue said, "And Larry?"

"Yeah, boss."

"Don't disappoint me."

*   *   *

Outside, Larry Rhodes was thinking that he had no intention of disappointing his boss. He'd been wanting to take Bo Simmons on himself for a long time. Bo had a reputation as a rough man, good with his gun and with his fists. In fact Rhodes knew he *was*, because he had seen Bo take on as many as three men by himself. Hell, if Canyon O'Grady hadn't come along and butted in, maybe ol' Bo would have been able to take all *five* of Purdue's men last night. Now, however, with ten men behind him, Rhodes knew that Bo was finished—and so was Canyon O'Grady. And with Bo dead, Buck Simmons would be otherwise occupied and wouldn't be able to stop Purdue from taking over his ranch.

Of course, Rhodes had no idea how Purdue expected to win Julia Simmons after that had been done, but his boss's love life wasn't his problem.

Right now he had only one problem. Canyon O'Grady wasn't even that important. He would just be a bonus. The one problem right now was Bo Simmons, plain and simple, and it was a problem Larry Rhodes was going to handle the *right* way.

24

"You're a fox," Canyon O'Grady said to Bo Simmons.

"What?"

"I just figured out why you wanted to ride into town today," O'Grady said, "just you and me. I don't know why I didn't see it before. I must be getting old."

"Don't tell *me* about getting old," Bo grumbled into his beer. "But tell me why I wanted to come into town."

"You're setting us up as targets," O'Grady said. "You *want* Purdue to try for us again."

"Why would I set you up for that?" Bo asked.

"Because you see it as the only way to settle this," O'Grady said. "If Purdue sends men after us in broad daylight, then we'll be able to prove that he did send them after us. That is, if we live through it."

"I don't think I'm that smart," Bo said, but the look on his face was smug.

"Come on, Bo," O'Grady said. "How's the word going to get back to Purdue that we're here?"

Bo stared into his beer for a few moments, then set it down, folded his hands over his belly, and looked across the table at O'Grady.

"You sent a telegram, didn't you?"

"Yeah," O'Grady said, "so?"

"Purdue's got the operator on his payroll."

"You know that for a fact?"

"Got to be," Bo said. "That's why he was able to cut into some of Buck's deals, because he knew about them in advance. He undercut us on a big horse sale, and could only have gotten the information from the telegraph office."

"So once I sent my telegram, the operator would send him word that we were here, right?"

"Right."

"And we're just sitting here waiting for them to come?" O'Grady asked.

"Right."

"There'll be more of them this time, you know."

"I know," Bo said, "but we did pretty good last night, and this time we know they're coming."

"If we know they're coming," O'Grady said, "we should get set up for them."

"What do you mean?"

"I mean finish that beer and follow me. . . ."

Gill was surprised when O'Grady and Bo Simmons reentered his room so soon.

"I thought you guys weren't comin' back until afternoon."

"That's obvious," O'Grady said, staring at the naked girl in bed with Gill.

She was easy to spot. When they walked in she was crouched down between Gill's legs with her full, round bottom hiked up into the air while she worked on him with her mouth. They could see bushy black hair between her legs. Now she looked back at them sheepishly over her shoulder.

"This is, uh, Karen from the saloon," Gill said. "She's been, uh, keepin' me company."

"You about done?" Bo asked.

"About."

Bo looked at O'Grady, who said, "Okay, we'll wait in the hall."

Moments later Karen came out fully dressed, gave them a saucy grin, and hip-twitched her way down the hall to the stairs. O'Grady and Bo went back into the room to find a smiling Gill waiting for them in bed.

"I guess you're feelin' better," Bo said.

"Some."

"Well enough to handle a rifle?" O'Grady asked.

"Sure," Gill said, frowning, "if I have to. What have you got in mind?"

O'Grady looked at Bo, who motioned for him to go ahead.

"Listen. . . ."

When they stepped out of the hotel, Vince Gill was propped up in his hotel window with his rifle across his lap, waiting.

"Do you know anyone else in town who might be of help?" O'Grady asked.

"No," Bo said, "nobody who would go against Will Purdue."

"Bo," O'Grady asked, "why didn't we just bring some of your men with us?"

"Well, for one thing, my brother would never want to put guns into the hands of his men," Bo said. "He says he hired them to work the ranch, not to fire a gun."

155.

"But anybody who hires on to work a ranch knows he might have to fight to protect it someday."

"That's the way I feel about it," Bo said. "But remember, it's my brother's ranch—and if push came to snove . . . I mean, if it actually came down to fighting or losing the ranch, I think Buck would leave it up to each individual man."

"Give them the choice of fighting or moving on, you mean?"

"Yeah."

"And if that happened?" O'Grady asked. "You know your men. How many of them would fight?"

"About half," Bo said. "And maybe half of *them* would actually be able to hit what they were aiming at. No, if we can do this, and show the sheriff that Purdue was behind it, I think I'll be able to get him off of Buck's back."

"Without risking Buck's life, or Mark's, or Julia's, huh?"

"That's right."

"Just yours."

"Right again."

"And mine."

Bo gave O'Grady a guilty look.

"You're right, Canyon," he said, shaking his head. "I didn't have any right to pull you into this. I should give you the same choice I'd give my men. Fight, or move on. Well okay, then, I'm givin' it to you."

O'Grady didn't hesitate.

"I'd have to stay behind and help you fight, Bo."

"Why?"

"Hey," O'Grady said, "I'm wearing your brother's boots."

"What's that got to do with it?"

O'Grady shrugged and said, "It's as good a reason as any, isn't it? Besides, if I *tried* to run in these boots I'd end up falling on my face."

"Well then," Bo said, "why don't you go and buy yourself a new pair?"

"That sounds like a damn good idea, Bo, except for one thing."

"What's that?"

"My foot is still too swollen for me to buy a pair in my own size."

"Well then, we might as well go back to the saloon and wait."

They crossed the street and walked to the saloon, turning first to look up at the hotel. Vince Gill waved at them from the window of his room.

Again they were sitting at a table, with a beer each. It was later in the afternoon, but the place wasn't filled much more than it had been before. It was quiet, too, so quiet that they heard the sound of a couple of horses riding into town.

"That can't be them," Bo said. "Less'n they're comin' in one or two at a time."

"Take a look," O'Grady said, pulling Buck Simmons' boots back on.

Bo stood, walked to the batwing doors, and looked outside.

"Uh-oh," he said, turning his head to look at O'Grady over his shoulder, "we're in trouble now."

"Is it them?"

"Worse," Bo said, turning to face O'Grady. "It's my brother Buck."

25

"And he's comin' this way!" Bo continued.

He turned and hurried back to the table with O'Grady. He was sitting by the time Buck walked in, with Julia.

"Bo."

Bo half stood, and pointed at Julia.

"What's she doin' here?"

"The question is," Buck said, "what are *you two* doin' here? No, don't answer that. I *know* what you're doin' here, and you're crazy. Come on back to the ranch."

"Can't, Buck," Bo said. "We got work to do."

Buck looked at O'Grady and asked, "You're in on this, then?"

"Let's just say that I eventually volunteered," O'Grady said. He looked past Buck and caught Julia's eye.

"So tell me, you fellas just figure to sit around town waiting for Will Purdue to send some men after you?"

"He did it last night," Bo said. "He's gettin' tired of waitin, Buck. He's impatient. *You* were always the one told me that an impatient man is a careless man."

"Don't be throwing my own quotes back in my face, Bo," Buck said. "Besides, there's no guarantee that he'll send anyone today. I mean, how does he even know that you're in town?"

Bo pointed at O'Grady and said, "He sent a telegraph message when we got here."

Buck looked at O'Grady and said, "Did you say you'd be waiting for an answer?"

"Yes."

"You know the key operator works for Purdue," Bo said to his brother.

Buck rubbed a hand over his face, then turned and looked at his daughter.

"Go back to the ranch, Julia."

"Oh, no," Julia said, moving up so she was standing right next to her father. "If you're staying to take part in this craziness, so am I."

"Buck," Bo said, "make her go home."

Buck looked at Bo and said, "You know your niece, *Uncle* Bo, *you* make her go home.

Bo looked at Julia and said, "Go home, girl!"

"No."

He looked at O'Grady and said, "I tried."

"Can you shoot?" O'Grady asked her.

"Pistol *and* rifle."

O'Grady did her the courtesy of not looking at her father or uncle for confirmation.

"We have Vince Gill positioned at his window in the hotel," O'Grady said, looking at Buck. "If we put Julia across the street we'll have them in a crossfire."

"Sounds good," Buck said.

"I want to be down here with you," Julia said.

"Bo and I will be on the ground, in plain sight," O'Grady said. "Buck, why don't you put Julia in place, and then find someplace to hide yourself. When they do ride in, it'll be better if they only see us."

"All right," Buck said. "Bo, you pushed this."

Bo put both hands up and said, "I didn't push nothin', Buck. I *been* pushed, now all I'm doin' is pushin' back."

Buck paused, rubbed his hand over his face, and then said, "Maybe you're right. Maybe it *is* time to do some pushing back, especially after what they pulled last night."

"Maybe," Bo said, "just maybe, we can get it all settled today."

"Maybe," Buck said, but he didn't sound so sure.

"Better get into position, Buck," O'Grady said.

"Yeah," Buck agreed. He turned and said to Julia, "Come on, girl."

"We'd better go and sit outside, where we can be seen, Bo."

"Right."

Everybody was moving except Julia.

"Julia?" her father said.

"Pa, could you and Uncle Bo go outside? I want to talk to Canyon for a minute."

Buck looked from O'Grady to his daughter and then said, "All right, but don't take too long."

"I won't."

Buck and Bo went outside, and Julia followed their progress until they were out the batwing doors.

"Julia . . ."

She whirled on him, closed the distance between them, threw her arms around his neck, and kissed him. It was a hard kiss, at first, and then it softened, her mouth opening to accept his tongue. She pressed her body tightly against his and they stood that way a very long time. The bartender stopped what he was doing, leaned on the bar, and just watched.

When she broke the kiss, she was breathless and her color was high.

"Julia . . ." he said again, but she didn't give him a chance to say anything more than her name.

"If you get killed," she said to him, "I will *never* forgive you. Just remember that," she said, kissing him shortly this time and pressing against him again, "and be careful. When this is all over, you and I have an appointment."

"Julia . . ." he began again, but she turned and ran to the doors, then slowed and walked out as if nothing had happened.

O'Grady, momentarily stunned, looked over at the bartender, who smiled and wiggled his eyebrows.

O'Grady just shrugged and walked from the saloon.

Buck and Julia were crossing the street together, and as O'Grady came out Bo looked at him curiously.

"What did she want?"

O'Grady looked at Bo and said, "She wanted to tell me to be careful."

"She had to get you alone to do that?" he asked.

"She wanted to tell me to be *real* careful," O'Grady said.

"Oh," Bo said, and then, "Ohhh," as if he had just realized something. Then he frowned, looked at O'Grady, and said, "Why?"

"Never mind," O'Grady said. "Let's get a couple of chairs and sit."

They found a couple of straight-backed wooden chairs, set them against the front wall of the saloon, and sat down. From there they'd be able to watch both sides of the street. Normally they would expect someone coming from the Simmons ranch *or* the Purdue ranch to ride into town from the north, but they would be well aware if someone rode in from the south.

"They might figure that we're waitin' for them and come from the south," Bo said.

"Do you really think they'd think that *two* men were waiting to ambush *them*?" O'Grady asked.

"I guess not," Bo said, but they both agreed that they'd keep their eye out both ways, just to play it safe.

An hour later, Bo took a stroll across the street. The hotel was on the same side of the street as the saloon, so from where they were sitting they couldn't see Vince Gill's window.

When Bo returned and sat down next to O'Grady he said, "Gill's still awake."

From where they sat they were able to see the window Julie was sitting at. She waved, and O'Grady simply nodded his head.

Neither O'Grady nor Bo knew where Buck was.

"He's well hidden," O'Grady said.

"Buck can do that," Bo said. "If he hadn't wanted so bad to become a rancher, him and me, we could have raised some hell together."

"So you went out and raised hell all by yourself, huh?" O'Grady asked.

"For a while," Bo said. "Buck says that was my wasted youth, but I had a good time and I learned a lot."

"What did you learn?"

Bo looked at O'Grady and said, "Mostly, I learned that I wasted my youth."

"Well, my guess is you're making up for it now,"

O'Grady said. "Can I ask you something, just out of curiosity?"

"Sure."

"Do you own a piece of the ranch?"

"No," Bo said, "it's all Buck's."

"How come?"

"He offered me a piece," Bo said with a shrug. "I didn't earn it. *He* built that place up without me. Why should I come riding in later and accept a piece for nothing?"

"Because you're family?"

"No," Bo said, shaking his head, "I couldn't do that, Canyon. I took the job as foreman. That I thought I could prove I deserved, and I have."

"Ever think about getting your own ranch?"

"No." There was no hesitation.

"Why not?"

"Paperwork."

"What?"

"When you own your own ranch there's a lot more involved than just working it," Bo said. "Paperwork is one of those things. I don't think I'd be good at any of that other stuff. I can work the ranch, though, so it makes sense for me to be a foreman."

They both stopped short as something small landed on the boardwalk on front of them.

"What the—" Bo said.

Again, something struck the wood at their feet. O'Grady bent down and picked it up. It was a bean.

And a third one.

"They're coming," O'Grady said. "Wherever your brother is, he's throwing beans at us to tell us they're coming."

"He must be in the general store," Bo said.

"Or above it," O'Grady said. As the sound of horses came to them he added, "It doesn't matter, though. They're here."

"Good," Bo said, standing up, "let's get this over with."

26

As O'Grady stood up from his chair he said to Bo, "We've got to keep them in the middle of the street."

"That means *we'll* have to be in the middle of the street," Bo said.

"Yeah," O'Grady said, "but we can't start anything. We have to let them make the first move."

Other people on the street, hearing the approach of a large group of horses, sensed that something was wrong. They shrank back from the street, but did not go inside. If something was going to happen, they certainly didn't want to miss *seeing* it.

"Okay," O'Grady said, "let's time this right. Just as they come into sight, we'll start crossing the street."

"Let's just hope they don't start shooting as soon as they see us," Bo said.

"Thanks for alerting me to that possibility."

Both men watched and waited. The sound became louder, and then they could see the riders. Nine . . . ten . . . eleven, O'Grady counted.

"Eleven?" he said.

"That's what I got."

"Let's go," O'Grady said, and stepped down.

* * *

Larry Rhodes saw the two men crossing the street ahead of him and his ten men, and he *knew* that it was Bo Simmons and Canyon O'Grady.

What luck! he thought, but he refrained from drawing his gun and firing immediately. He'd wait until he could see the look on Bo Simmons' face.

O'Grady and Bo Simmons reached the center of the street and stopped, as if curious about the approaching riders. O'Grady wished that they'd had even more time to get set up, but that kind of thinking was useless now. They just had to go with what they had.

"I feel naked," Bo Simmons said, "standing out here in the middle of the street like this."

O'Grady looked at him briefly, then at the approaching riders.

"When the shooting starts," he said to Bo, reminding him, "you go left and I'll go right."

"Right. I'll take Rhodes," Bo said, recognizing the foreman.

O'Grady briefly glanced off to his right, to where he had secreted his rifle. Similarly, Bo's rifle was across the street to the left. For them to be standing in the middle of the street holding their rifles would have been a giveaway that they were expecting trouble.

The riders got to within twenty feet of them, and then Larry Rhodes halted their progress with a raised hand.

"Afternoon, Bo," he said.

"Larry."

"Looks like you boys are in our way," Rhodes said. "Want to step aside?"

"Sure, Larry," Bo said. "Hey, the last thing we want is to be in your way."

"You mean like your brother is in Will's way?"

166

"Is that a fact, Larry?" Bo asked. "You know, my brother sort of feels that there's room here for everyone. How come Purdue don't feel the same way?"

"Will's a realistic man, Bo," Rhodes said. "He knows there's only room for one *big* rancher in the area. He also knows who that should be. Why don't you get your brother to sell out, Bo?"

"Can't do it, Larry," Bo said. "Sorry, but my brother is not only as ugly as a goat, he's as stubborn."

"That's too bad," Rhodes said. "He's gonna lose everything, then."

"No he ain't, Larry," Bo said. "Not while I'm alive."

"That can be taken care of, Bo," Rhodes said.

Bo smiled and said, "Take your best shot, Larry."

"You're a dead man, Bo," Rhodes said, and drew his gun while he was still talking.

Bo was ready for him, though, and he drew faster and fired. The bullet struck Rhodes in the right shoulder, and a look of surprise came over his face just before he fell from his horse.

O'Grady drew and shot the man just to Rhodes' right, and then everyone was drawing his gun.

Bo and O'Grady hit the ground and rolled left and right as Rhodes' men began to fire.

At the same time Gill, Julia, and Buck started firing, and Rhodes' men realized they were in a crossfire.

O'Grady fired his handgun a few more times before holstering it and picking up his rifle. He fired as quickly as he could eject the spent shells, and across the street Bo did the same.

The element of surprise was everything. Half of Rhodes' men were confused, and the other half were firing at random.

167

By the time one of them got the smart idea of throwing *down* his gun and *up* his hands there were only three others left to follow his lead.

Suddenly, a deafening silence fell over the scene. O'Grady and Bo stood up and stepped back into the street, keeping their rifles on the four remaining men.

"Get down off your horses!" Bo shouted.

The four men complied. By this time Buck was in the street with them, and he directed the four men over to a store wall and told them to face it.

O'Grady and Bo checked the men who were lying in the street. They were all dead, except for Larry Rhodes. He stared up at them from the ground, his hand clutching his shoulder.

"You were expecting us?" he asked, through the pain.

"Sure we were, Larry," Bo said.

"H-how?"

"Your boss, Larry," Bo said. "He's just so damned predictable."

"Here comes the sheriff," O'Grady said.

"Sure," Bo said, "now that the shooting has stopped."

O'Grady looked down at Larry Rhodes and said, "Be smart, Rhodes. Don't go to jail all by yourself. This wasn't all your idea. Tell the sheriff that."

Rhodes scowled and looked away, but O'Grady could see that the man was thinking over what he had said.

"What's goin' on here?" Sheriff Zeke Harrison demanded.

"Zeke!" Bo cried expansively. "You're just in time! Mr. Rhodes here has somethin' he wants to tell you— don't you, Larry?"

"Jesus, Bo," Harrison said, looking around, "these men are all dead!"

"Except for those four," Bo said, pointing to the four men Buck Simmons was covering. "They'll probably have somethin' to tell you, too, about your Mr. Will Purdue." Bo lowered his rifle and stared at Harrison. "Time for you to *really* act like a sheriff, Zeke."

Harrison stared back, then pointed his gun at Larry Rhodes, and said, "All right, get up, Rhodes."

O'Grady and Bo walked over to where Buck was standing, to be joined moments later by an anxious-looking Julia.

"Everyone okay?" she asked.

"Don't know," Bo said, "let us check."

Bo looked himself over and found that he had taken a bullet in the left arm.

"Sonuvabitch!" he said. "I didn't even feel it."

"Bo!" Buck exclaimed, his real concern plain to see.

"I'm okay, Buck," Bo said. "I been shot before. I'll just get over to the doc's."

"Canyon?" Julia asked.

O'Grady had finished inspecting himself and said, "No hits." He looked at her father and said, "Buck?"

"They didn't even know where I was," Buck said. "Julia?"

"I'm fine, Papa."

Buck smiled.

O'Grady looked up at Vince Gill's window, and Gill smiled and waved back that he was all right.

"Looks like we're in one piece," O'Grady said, "for the most part."

"Luck," Bo said, "pure and simple."

"Luck?" Buck asked. "What was that remark about me being as ugly as a goat?"

"Uh, it was just somethin' to say, Buck," Bo said, grinning sheepishly. "No offense."

Buck glared at his brother, then softened his look and said, "None taken, brother."

"Will this keep Will Purdue off our backs now, Pa?" Julia asked.

"I don't know, girl," Buck said. "He'll have some explaining to do about sending eleven men after two. I guess we'll just have to wait and see. I better get Bo here over to the doc before he bleeds to death. Will you two be okay?" He looked at O'Grady and Julia in turn.

"We'll be fine," Julia said, giving O'Grady the eye.

As Buck and Bo walked away, Julia sidled up next to O'Grady and said, "We had an appointment."

"Now?" he asked, surprised.

"Oh yes," she said softly. "Right now."

O'Grady marveled at the change that came over Julia Simmons in bed. No longer was she the woman who could outride and outshoot most of the men who worked on her father's ranch. Now she was all woman, soft and sweet-smelling and eager.

They went to the hotel right from the street and O'Grady got his old room. Once they were inside Julia discarded her clothing quickly, followed closely by O'Grady. Their hands reached out for each other and they touched and explored for a long time before O'Grady lowered his head to kiss her breasts, lick and suck her nipples while she cradled his head and gasped, pulling them both down onto the bed.

She moved her legs, spreading them as he moved

170

between her thighs. First he used his mouth and tongue to bring her as much pleasure as he knew how. Her cries filled the room as she lifted herself to his mouth, her hands grabbing handfuls of the sheets until she finally threw them over her mouth to muffle her screams. . . . .

Then he moved up and positioned himself between her thighs. He kissed her and entered her at the same time. She bit his tongue painfully, but he ignored it. The other sensations were too good to bother with a moment of sharp pain and the taste of his own blood.

She slid her hands around him, running them down his back, rubbing his hips and then clutching at his buttocks while he worked in and out of her.

"Oh, God," she moaned. "Canyon O'Grady, what took you so long? Didn't you know . . . didn't you know right away that I wanted you?"

He answered her by covering her mouth with his, wetting her thoroughly with his kisses and thrusting into her harder and faster until finally he exploded into her and she screamed against his mouth.

Later, while they were lying together regaining their breath, there was a knock on the door.

"Who is it?" O'Grady asked.

"Uh, telegraph operator, Mr. O'Grady. I got that answer you were waiting for."

"Slide it under the door," O'Grady said.

"Uh, sure . . . okay," the man said.

O'Grady had no intention of getting out of bed just to tip the operator. After all, wasn't the man getting paid enough from Will Purdue?

"Aren't you going to read it?" Julia asked, snuggling her warm body against his.

"I don't have to," O'Grady said. "I know what it's going to say."

"What?"

"Oh, nothing for you to be concerned about," he said, holding her close.

"You'll be leaving tomorrow, won't you?" she asked.

"Yes," he said. He'd be only one day late getting to Hastings. How much could one day matter?

"Will you stay with me today?" she asked. "All day?"

"All day," he promised.

The telegram from Wheeler would remain on the floor all day, too.

There's an epidemic with 27 million victims. And no visible symptoms.

It's an epidemic of people who can't read.

Believe it or not, 27 million Americans are functionally illiterate, about one adult in five.

The solution to this problem is you... when you join the fight against illiteracy. So call the Coalition for Literacy at toll-free 1-800-228-8813 and volunteer.

Volunteer Against Illiteracy. The only degree you need is a degree of caring.